THE G♠MBLING SMURFS

Peyo

A **SMURFS** GRAPHIC NOVEL BY *Peyo*

WITH THE COLLABORATION OF
LUC PARTHOENS AND THIERRY CULLIFORD – SCRIPT
LUDO BORECKI – ART
NINE CULLIFORD – COLOR

PAPERCUTZ™
NEW YORK

SMURFS GRAPHIC NOVELS AVAILABLE FROM PAPERCUTZ™

1. THE PURPLE SMURFS
2. THE SMURFS AND THE MAGIC FLUTE
3. THE SMURF KING
4. THE SMURFETTE
5. THE SMURFS AND THE EGG
6. THE SMURFS AND THE HOWLIBIRD
7. THE ASTROSMURF
8. THE SMURF APPRENTICE
9. GARGAMEL AND THE SMURFS
10. THE RETURN OF THE SMURFETTE
11. THE SMURF OLYMPICS
12. SMURF VS. SMURF
13. SMURF SOUP
14. THE BABY SMURF
15. THE SMURFLINGS
16. THE AEROSMURF
17. THE STRANGE AWAKENING
    OF LAZY SMURF
18. THE FINANCE SMURF
19. THE JEWEL SMURFER
20. DOCTOR SMURF
21. THE WILD SMURF
22. THE SMURF MENACE
23. CAN'T SMURF PROGRESS
24. THE SMURF REPORTER
25. THE GAMBLING SMURFS

- THE SMURF CHRISTMAS
- FOREVER SMURFETTE
- SMURFS MONSTERS
- THE VILLAGE BEHIND THE WALL
- THE VILLAGE BEHIND THE WALL 2:
  THE BETRAYAL OF SMURFBLOSSOM

THE SMURFS 3 IN 1 #1
THE SMURFS 3 IN 1 #2

THE SMURFS graphic novels are available in paperback for $5.99 each and in hardcover for $10.99 each, except for THE SMURFS #21–#25, and THE VILLAGE BEHIND THE WALL, which are $7.99 each in paperback and $12.99 each in hardcover, at booksellers everywhere. THE SMURFS 3 IN 1 #1-2 are in paperback only for $14.99 each. You can also order online at papercutz.com. Or call 1-800-886-1223, Monday through Friday, 9 – 5 EST. MC, Visa, and AmEx accepted. To order by mail, please add $5.00 for postage and handling for first book ordered, $1.00 for each additional book and make check payable to NBM Publishing. Send to: Papercutz, 160 Broadway, Suite 700, East Wing, New York, NY 10038.

THE SMURFS graphic novels are also available digitally wherever e-books are sold.

PAPERCUTZ.COM

THE GAMBLING SMURFS

SMURF™ © Peyo - 2019 - Licensed through Lafig Belgium - www.smurf.com

English translation copyright © 2019 by Papercutz.
All rights reserved.

"The Gambling Smurfs"
BY PEYO
WITH THE COLLABORATION OF
LUC PARTHOENS AND THIERRY CULLIFORD FOR THE SCRIPT
LUDO BORECKI FOR ARTWORK
NINE CULLIFORD FOR COLOR.

"THE FLUTE SMURFERS"
BY PEYO
WITH THE COLLABORATION OF
LUC PARTHOENS AND THIERRY CULLIFORD FOR THE SCRIPT,
JEROEN DE CONINCK FOR ARTWORK,
NINE CULLIFORD FOR COLORS.

Joe Johnson, SMURFLATIONS
Léa Zimmerman, SMURFIC DESIGN
Bryan Senka, LETTERING SMURF ("THE GAMBLING SMURFS")
Janice Chiang, LETTERING SMURFETTE ("THE FLUTE SMURFERS")
Matt Murray, SMURF CONSULTANT
Karr Antunes, SMURF INTERN
Jeff Whitman, MANAGING SMURF
Jim Salicrup, SMURF-IN-CHIEF

HARDCOVER EDITION ISBN: 978-1-5458-0149-9
PAPERBACK EDITION ISBN: 978-1-5458-0357-8

PRINTED IN KOREA MAY 2019

Papercutz books may be purchased for business or promotional use. For information on bulk purchases please contact Macmillan Corporate and Premium Sales Department at (800) 221-7945 x5442.

DISTRIBUTED BY MACMILLAN
FIRST PAPERCUTZ PRINTING

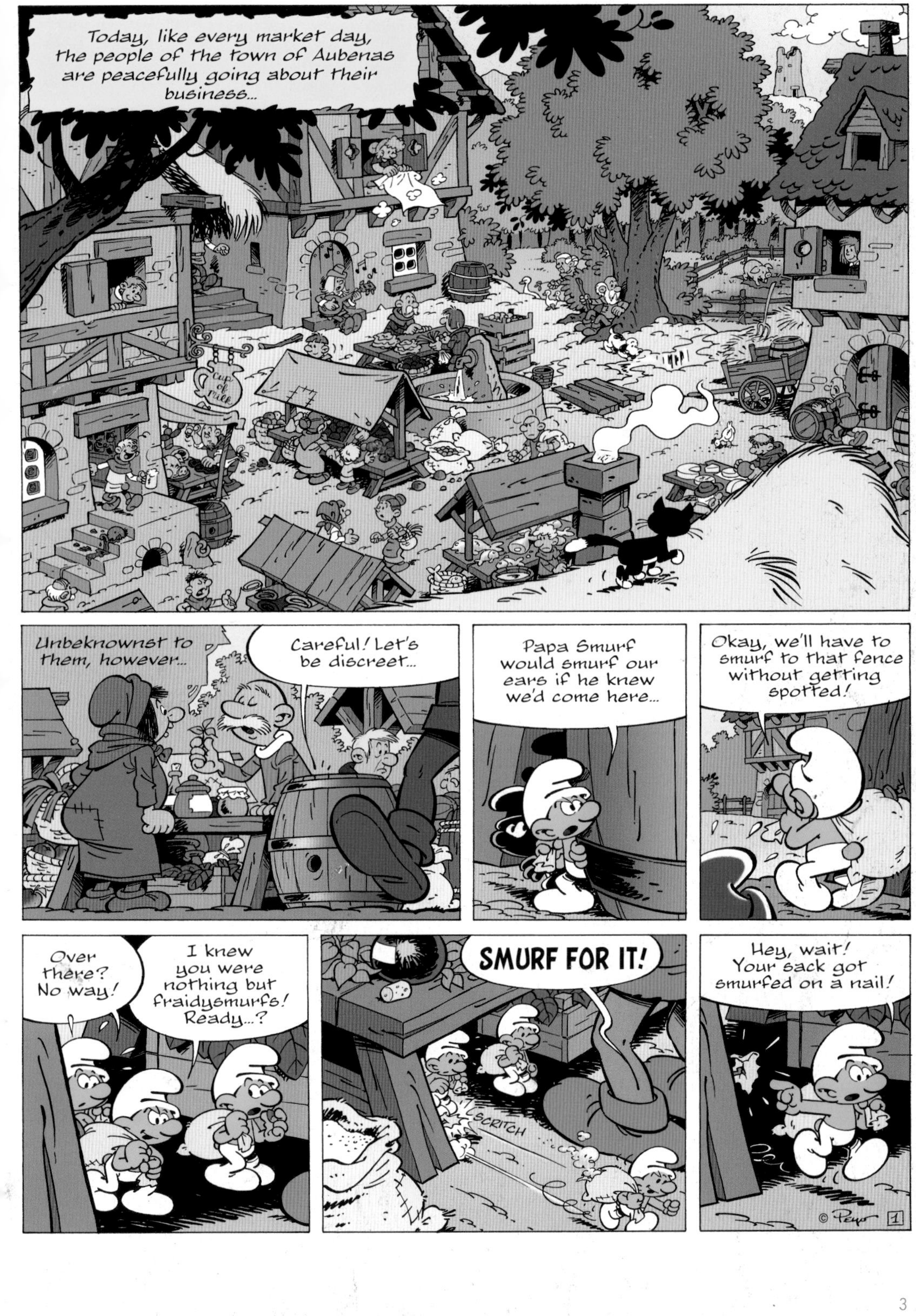

Today, like every market day, the people of the town of Aubenas are peacefully going about their business...
Cup of milk
Unbeknownst to them, however...
Careful! Let's be discreet...
Papa Smurf would smurf our ears if he knew we'd come here...
Okay, we'll have to smurf to that fence without getting spotted!
Over there? No way!
I knew you were nothing but fraidysmurfs! Ready...?
SMURF FOR IT!
SCRITCH
Hey, wait! Your sack got smurfed on a nail!
© Peyo
1

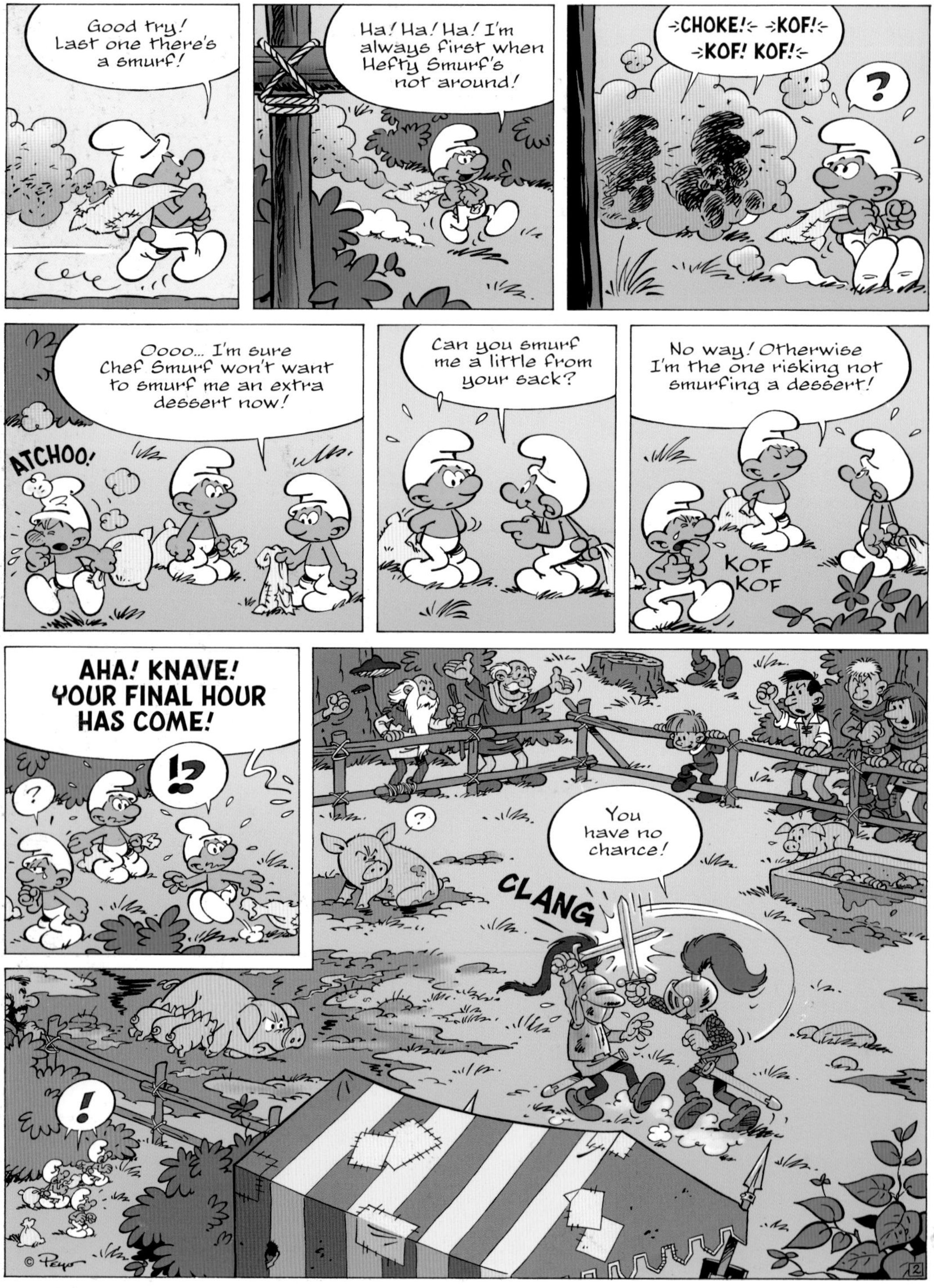

Good try! Last one there's a smurf!
Ha! Ha! Ha! I'm always first when Hefty Smurf's not around!
CHOKE! KOF! KOF! KOF!
?
Oooo... I'm sure Chef Smurf won't want to smurf me an extra dessert now!
ATCHOO!
Can you smurf me a little from your sack?
No way! Otherwise I'm the one risking not smurfing a dessert!
KOF KOF
AHA! KNAVE! YOUR FINAL HOUR HAS COME!
?
!?
?
You have no chance!
CLANG
!
© Peyo
2

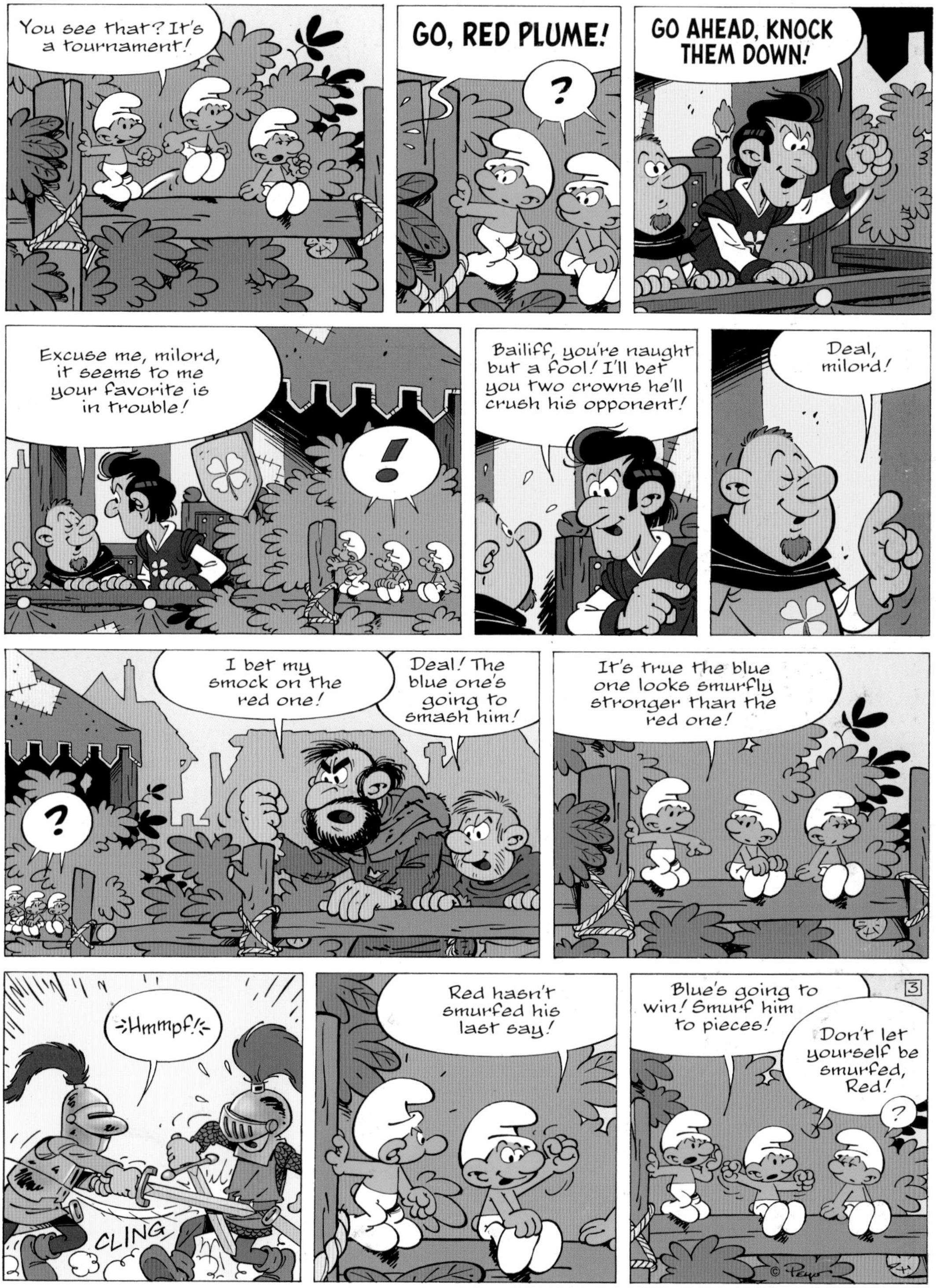
You see that? It's a tournament!
GO, RED PLUME!
?
GO AHEAD, KNOCK THEM DOWN!
Excuse me, milord, it seems to me your favorite is in trouble!
!
Bailiff, you're naught but a fool! I'll bet you two crowns he'll crush his opponent!
Deal, milord!
?
I bet my smock on the red one!
Deal! The blue one's going to smash him!
It's true the blue one looks smurfly stronger than the red one!
Hmmpf!
CLING
Red hasn't smurfed his last say!
3
Blue's going to win! Smurf him to pieces!
Don't let yourself be smurfed, Red!
?
© Peyo

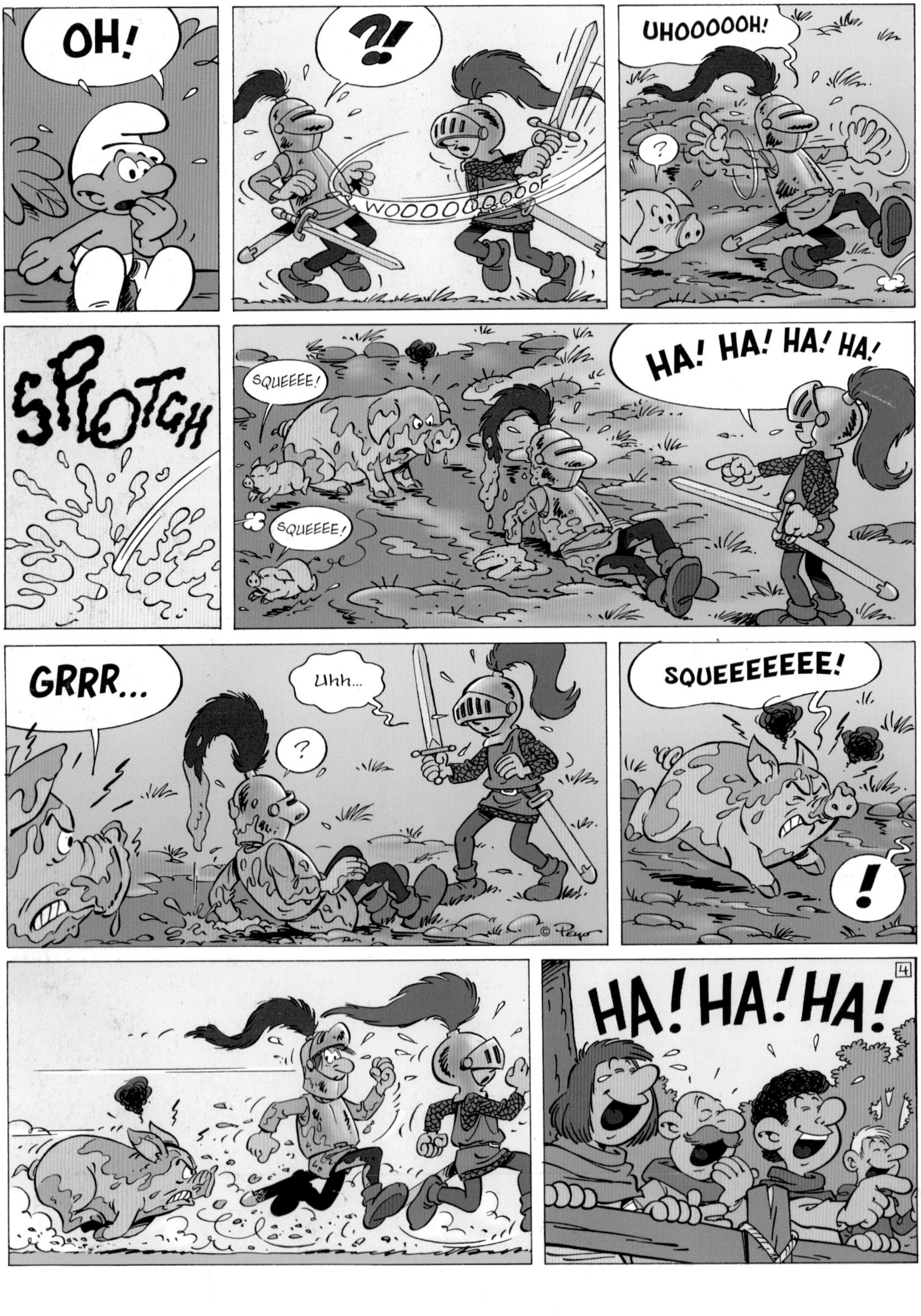
OH!
?!
WOOOOOOOOOF
UHOOOOOH!
?
SPLOTCH
SQUEEEE!
SQUEEEE!
HA! HA! HA! HA!
GRRR...
Uhh...
?
© Peyo
SQUEEEEEEE!
!
4
HA! HA! HA!

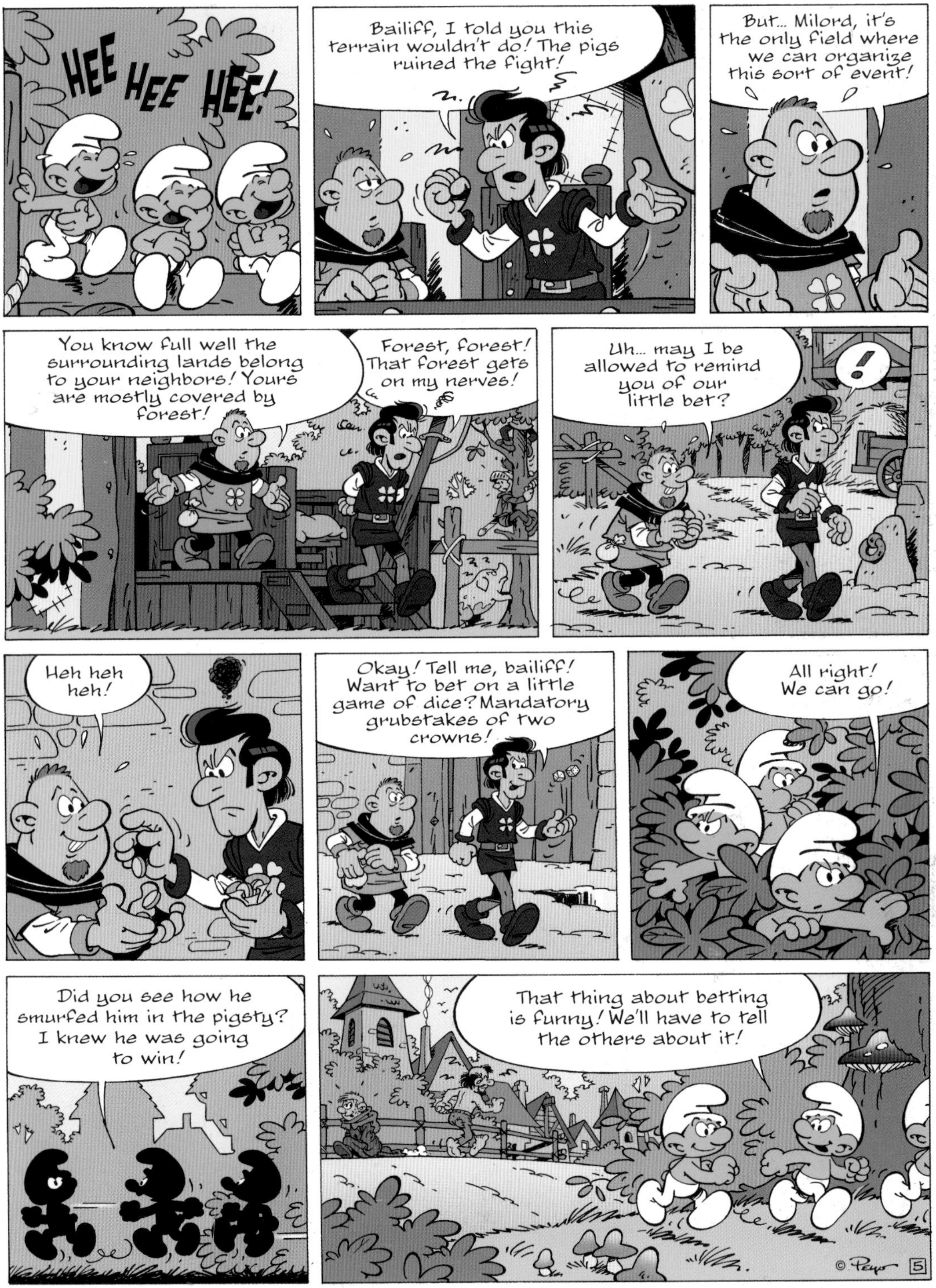
HEE HEE HEE!
Bailiff, I told you this terrain wouldn't do! The pigs ruined the fight!
But... Milord, it's the only field where we can organize this sort of event!
You know full well the surrounding lands belong to your neighbors! Yours are mostly covered by forest!
Forest, forest! That forest gets on my nerves!
Uh... may I be allowed to remind you of our little bet?
!
Heh heh heh!
Okay! Tell me, bailiff! Want to bet on a little game of dice? Mandatory grubstakes of two crowns!
All right! We can go!
Did you see how he smurfed him in the pigsty? I knew he was going to win!
That thing about betting is funny! We'll have to tell the others about it!
© Peyo
5

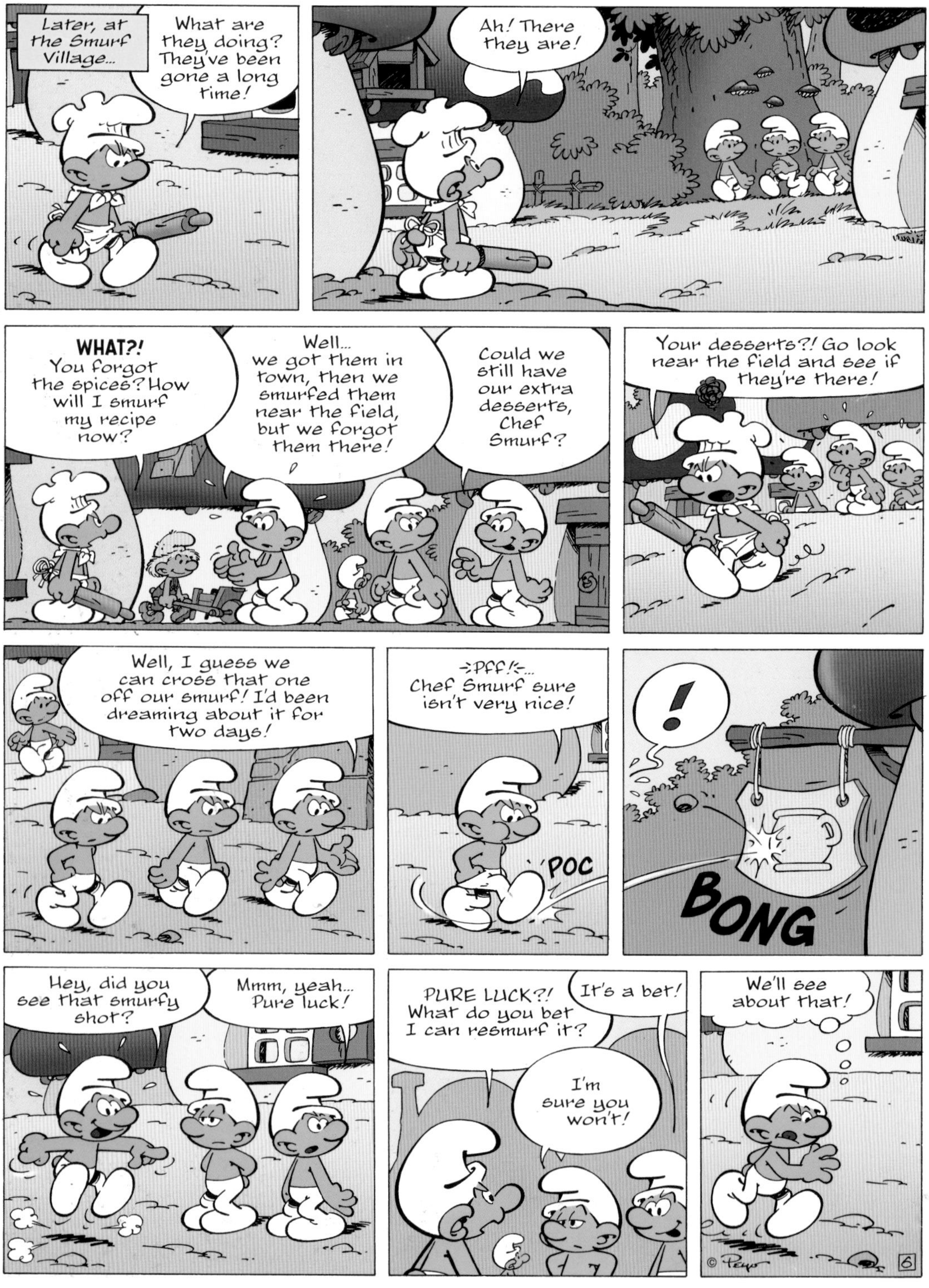
Later, at the Smurf Village...
What are they doing? They've been gone a long time!
Ah! There they are!
WHAT?! You forgot the spices? How will I smurf my recipe now?
Well... we got them in town, then we smurfed them near the field, but we forgot them there!
Could we still have our extra desserts, Chef Smurf?
Your desserts?! Go look near the field and see if they're there!
Well, I guess we can cross that one off our smurf! I'd been dreaming about it for two days!
PFF!... Chef Smurf sure isn't very nice!
POC
!
BONG
Hey, did you see that smurfy shot?
Mmm, yeah... Pure luck!
PURE LUCK?! What do you bet I can resmurf it?
It's a bet!
I'm sure you won't!
We'll see about that!
© Peyo
6

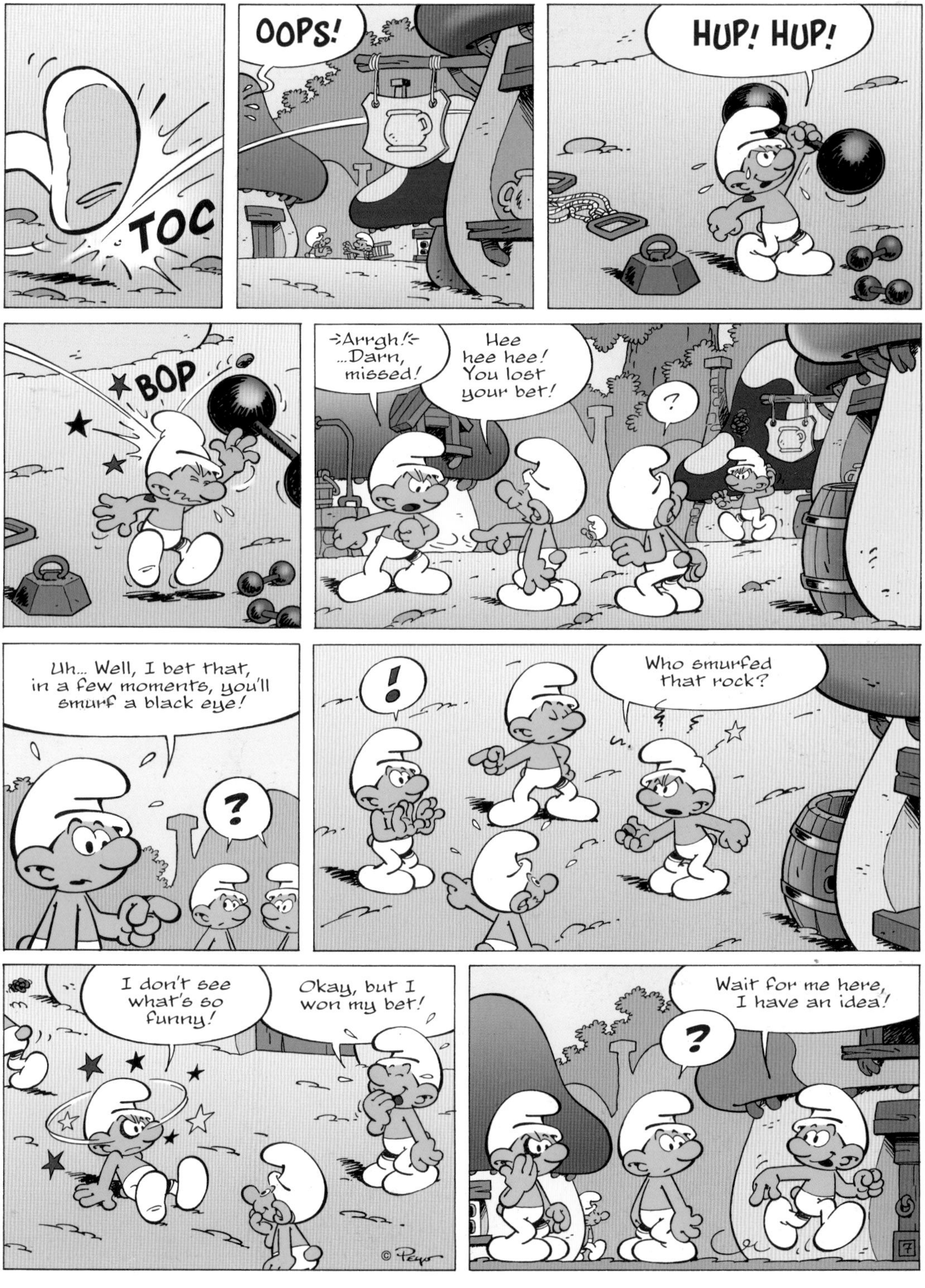
TOC
OOPS!
HUP! HUP!
BOP
Arrgh! ...Darn, missed!
Hee hee hee! You lost your bet!
?
Uh... Well, I bet that, in a few moments, you'll smurf a black eye!
?
!
Who smurfed that rock?
I don't see what's so funny!
Okay, but I won my bet!
© Peyo
?
Wait for me here, I have an idea!
7

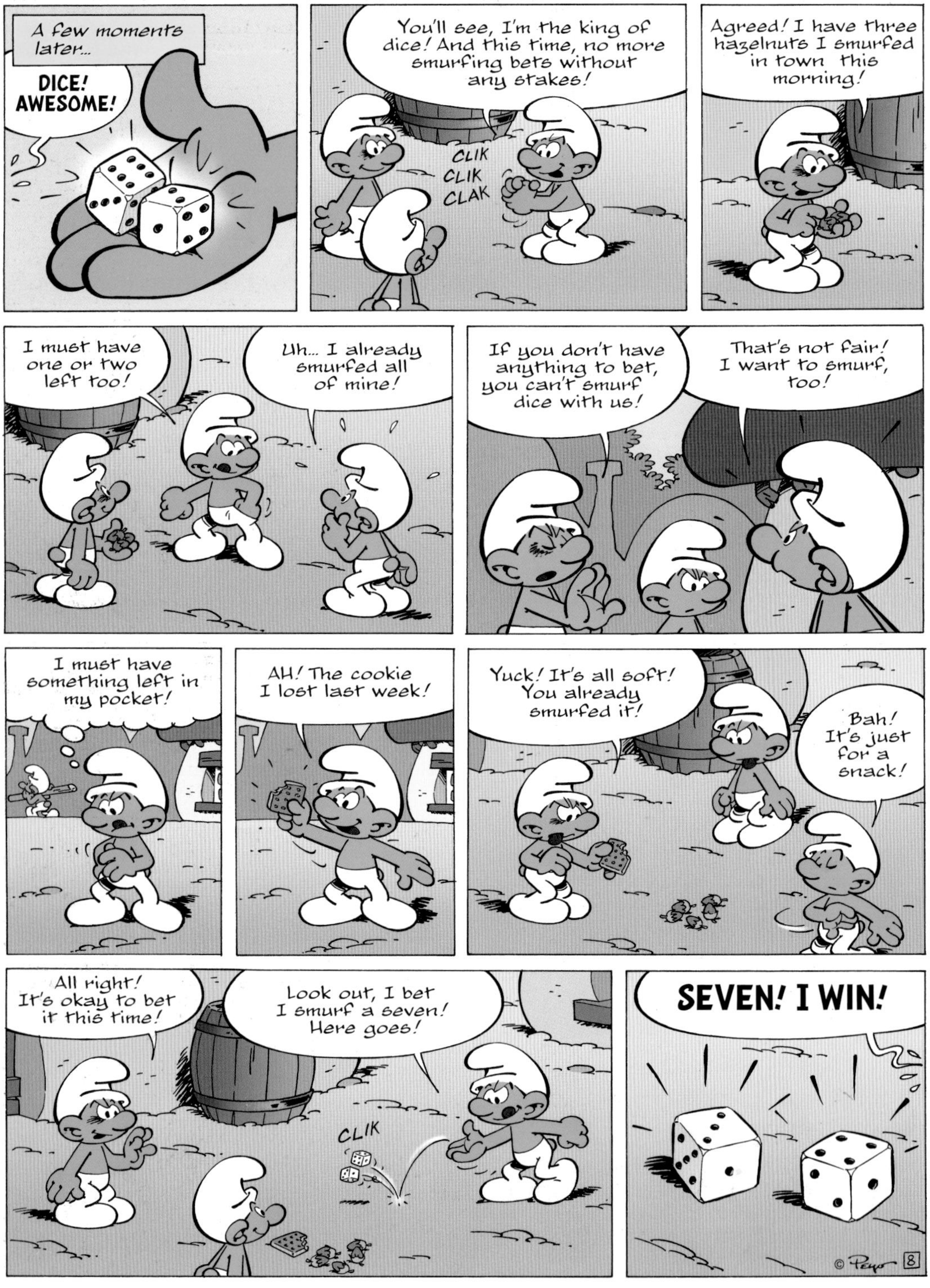

A few moments later...
DICE! AWESOME!
You'll see, I'm the king of dice! And this time, no more smurfing bets without any stakes!
CLIK CLIK CLAK
Agreed! I have three hazelnuts I smurfed in town this morning!
I must have one or two left too!
Uh... I already smurfed all of mine!
If you don't have anything to bet, you can't smurf dice with us!
That's not fair! I want to smurf, too!
I must have something left in my pocket!
AH! The cookie I lost last week!
Yuck! It's all soft! You already smurfed it!
Bah! It's just for a snack!
All right! It's okay to bet it this time!
Look out, I bet I smurf a seven! Here goes!
CLIK
SEVEN! I WIN!
© Peyo 8

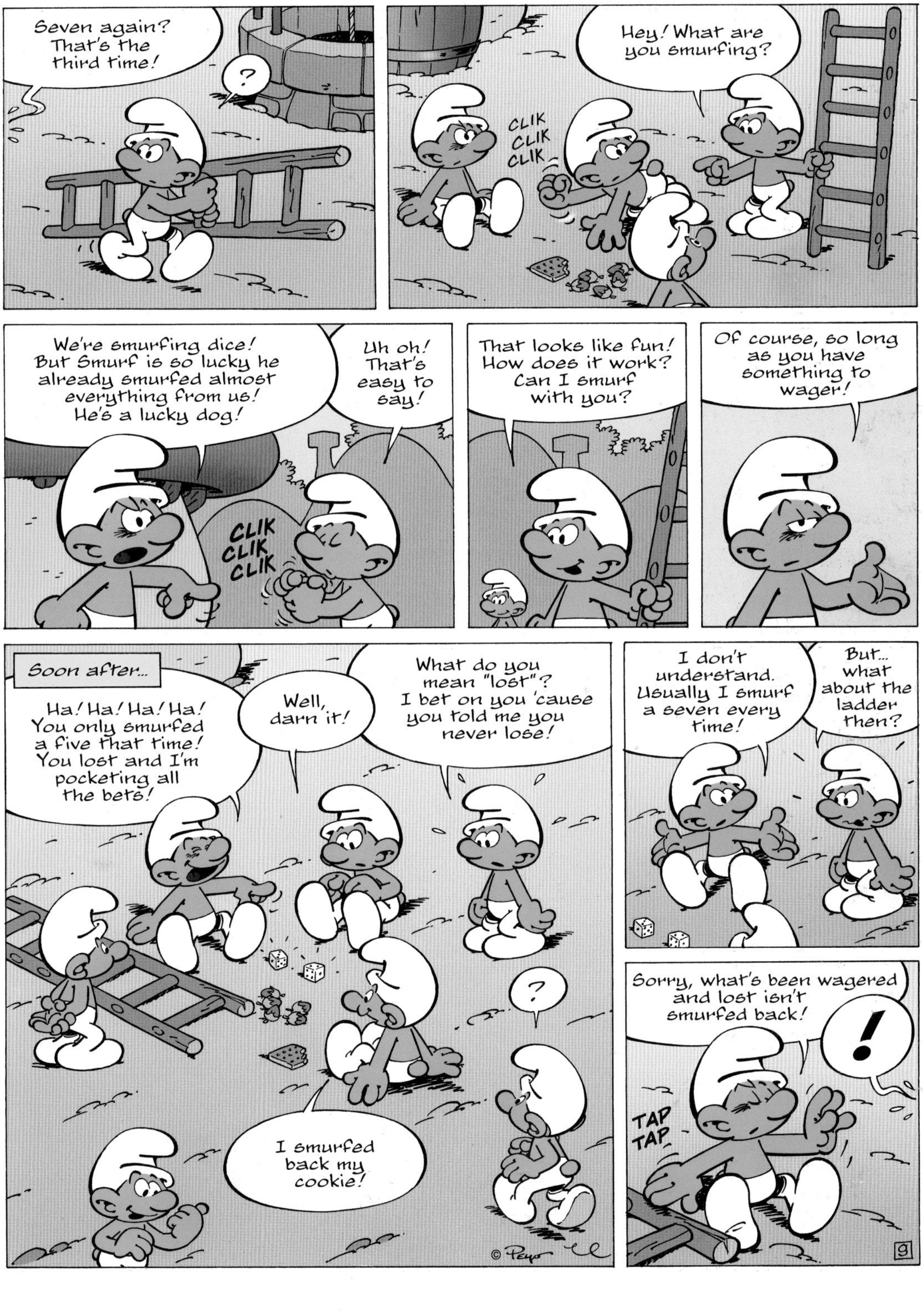

Seven again? That's the third time!
?
Hey! What are you smurfing?
CLIK CLIK CLIK
We're smurfing dice! But Smurf is so lucky he already smurfed almost everything from us! He's a lucky dog!
Uh oh! That's easy to say!
CLIK CLIK CLIK
That looks like fun! How does it work? Can I smurf with you?
Of course, so long as you have something to wager!
Soon after...
Ha! Ha! Ha! Ha! You only smurfed a five that time! You lost and I'm pocketing all the bets!
Well, darn it!
What do you mean "lost"? I bet on you 'cause you told me you never lose!
?
I smurfed back my cookie!
© Peyo
I don't understand. Usually I smurf a seven every time!
But... what about the ladder then?
Sorry, what's been wagered and lost isn't smurfed back!
!
TAP TAP
9

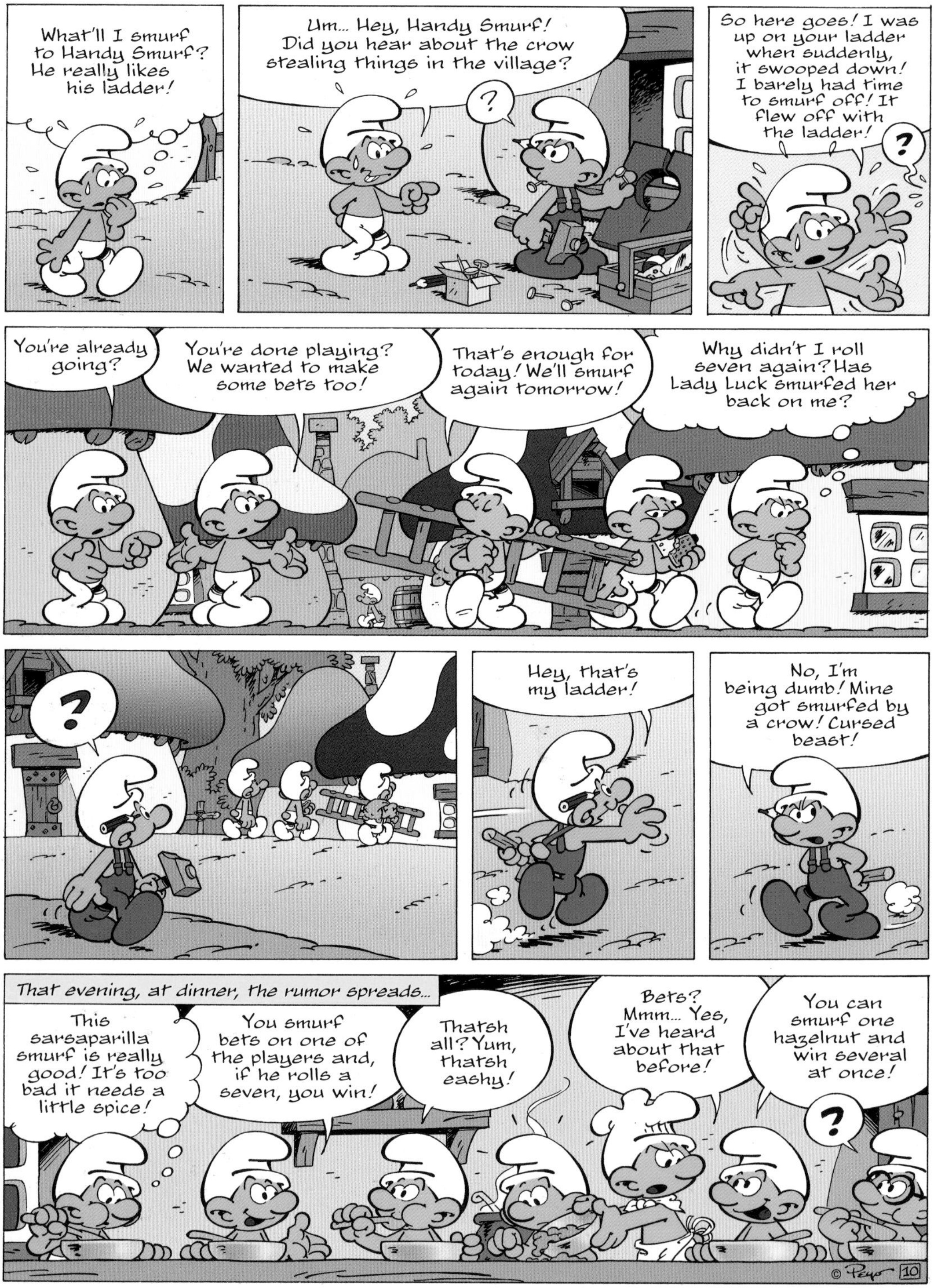

What'll I smurf to Handy Smurf? He really likes his ladder!
Um... Hey, Handy Smurf! Did you hear about the crow stealing things in the village?
?
So here goes! I was up on your ladder when suddenly, it swooped down! I barely had time to smurf off! It flew off with the ladder!
?
You're already going?
You're done playing? We wanted to make some bets too!
That's enough for today! We'll smurf again tomorrow!
Why didn't I roll seven again? Has Lady Luck smurfed her back on me?
?
Hey, that's my ladder!
No, I'm being dumb! Mine got smurfed by a crow! Cursed beast!
That evening, at dinner, the rumor spreads...
This sarsaparilla smurf is really good! It's too bad it needs a little spice!
You smurf bets on one of the players and, if he rolls a seven, you win!
Thatsh all? Yum, thatsh eashy!
Bets? Mmm... Yes, I've heard about that before!
You can smurf one hazelnut and win several at once!
?
© Peyo
10

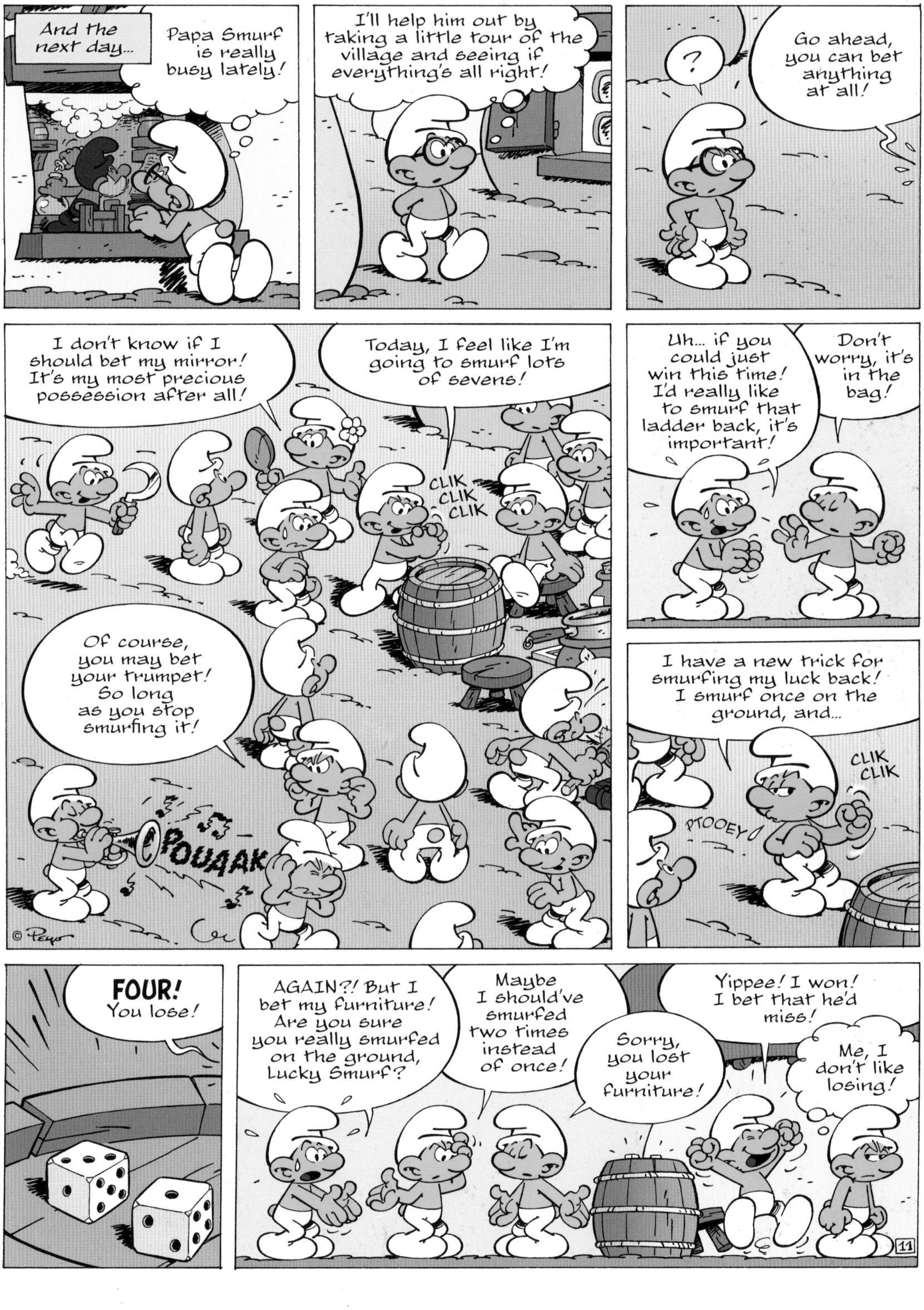
And the next day...
Papa Smurf is really busy lately!
I'll help him out by taking a little tour of the village and seeing if everything's all right!
?
Go ahead, you can bet anything at all!
I don't know if I should bet my mirror! It's my most precious possession after all!
Today, I feel like I'm going to smurf lots of sevens!
CLIK CLIK CLIK
Of course, you may bet your trumpet! So long as you stop smurfing it!
POUAAK
Uh... if you could just win this time! I'd really like to smurf that ladder back, it's important!
Don't worry, it's in the bag!
I have a new trick for smurfing my luck back! I smurf once on the ground, and...
CLIK CLIK
PTOOEY
FOUR! You lose!
AGAIN?! But I bet my furniture! Are you sure you really smurfed on the ground, Lucky Smurf?
Maybe I should've smurfed two times instead of once!
Sorry, you lost your furniture!
Yippee! I won! I bet that he'd miss!
Me, I don't like losing!
11

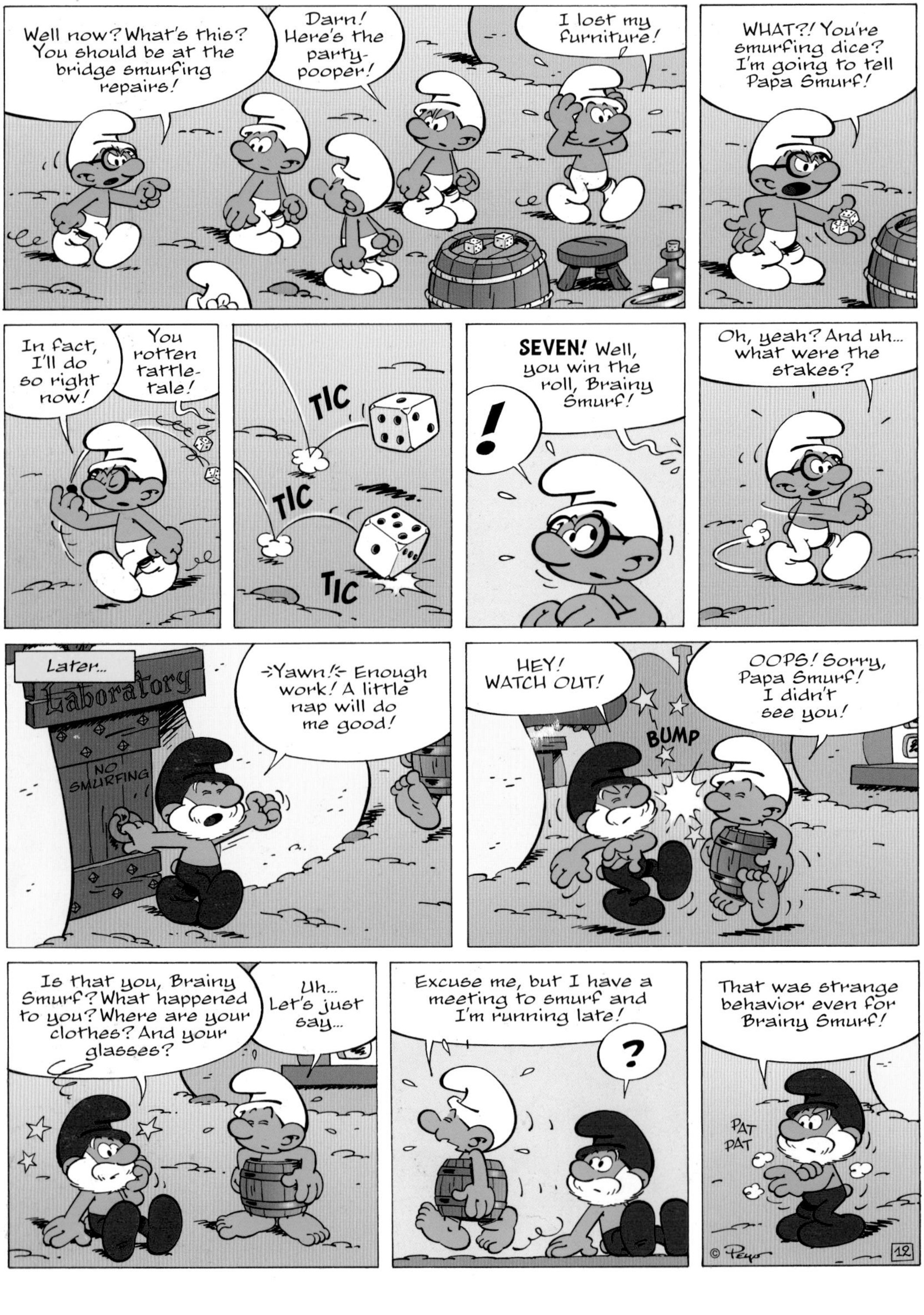
Well now? What's this? You should be at the bridge smurfing repairs!
Darn! Here's the party-pooper!
I lost my furniture!
WHAT?! You're smurfing dice? I'm going to tell Papa Smurf!
In fact, I'll do so right now!
You rotten tattle-tale!
TIC
TIC
TIC
SEVEN! Well, you win the roll, Brainy Smurf!
!
Oh, yeah? And uh... what were the stakes?
Later...
Laboratory
NO SMURFING
-Yawn!- Enough work! A little nap will do me good!
HEY! WATCH OUT!
OOPS! Sorry, Papa Smurf! I didn't see you!
BUMP
Is that you, Brainy Smurf? What happened to you? Where are your clothes? And your glasses?
Uh... Let's just say...
Excuse me, but I have a meeting to smurf and I'm running late!
?
That was strange behavior even for Brainy Smurf!
PAT PAT
© Peyo
12

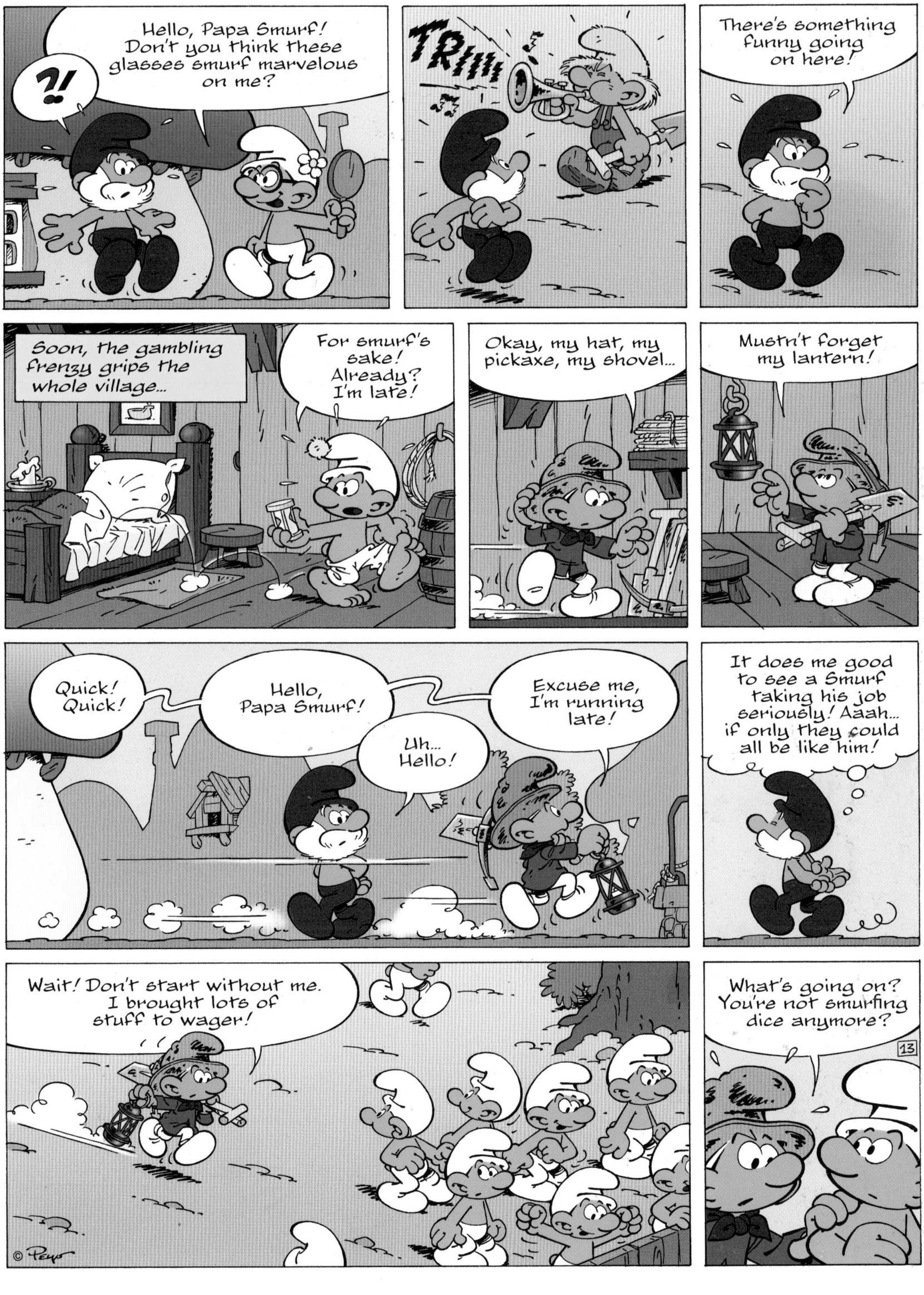
?!
Hello, Papa Smurf! Don't you think these glasses smurf marvelous on me?
TRIIII
There's something funny going on here!
Soon, the gambling frenzy grips the whole village...
For smurf's sake! Already? I'm late!
Okay, my hat, my pickaxe, my shovel...
Mustn't forget my lantern!
Quick! Quick!
Hello, Papa Smurf!
Uh... Hello!
Excuse me, I'm running late!
It does me good to see a Smurf taking his job seriously! Aaah... if only they could all be like him!
Wait! Don't start without me. I brought lots of stuff to wager!
What's going on? You're not smurfing dice anymore?
13
© Peyo

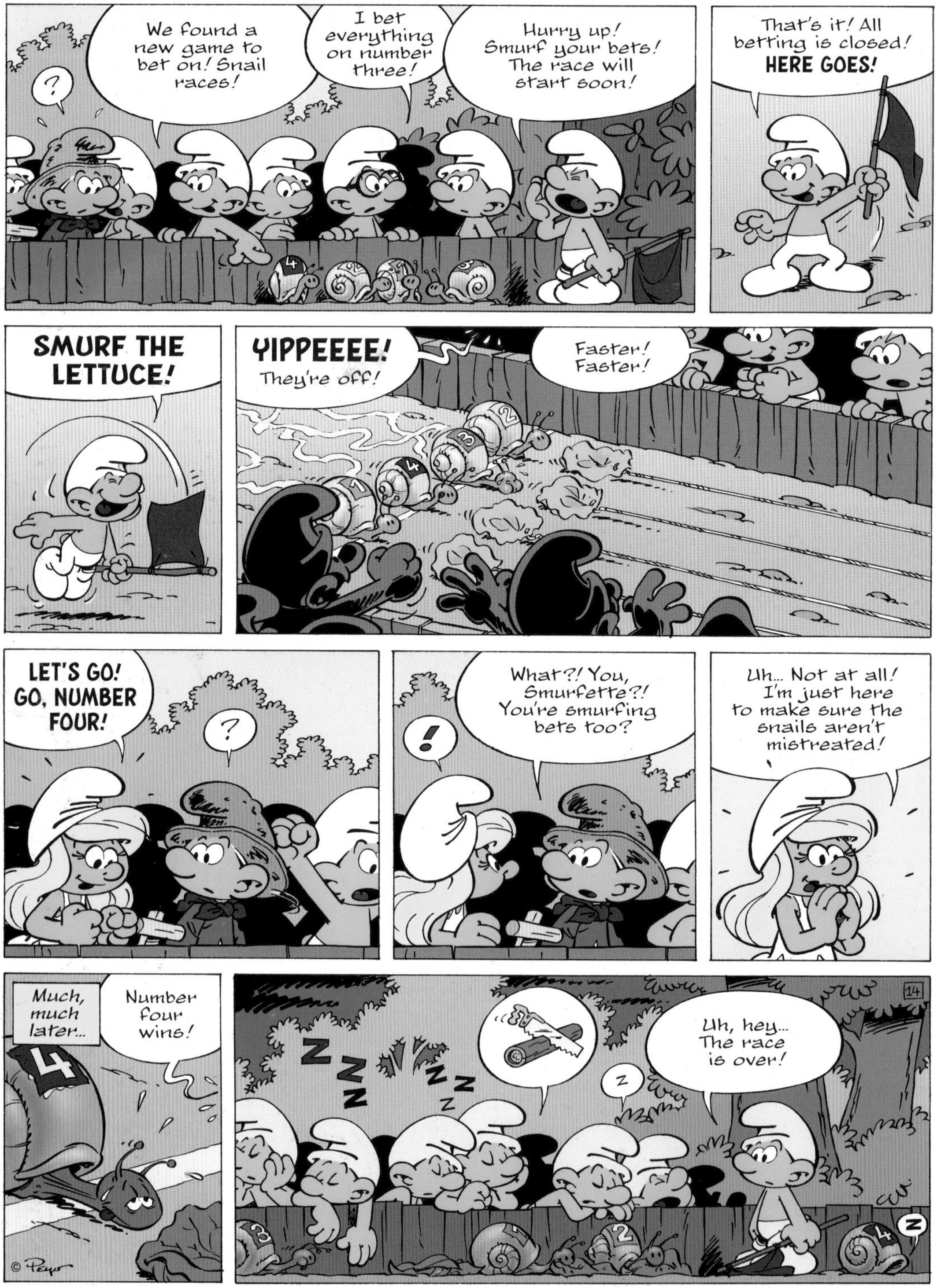
?
We found a new game to bet on! Snail races!
I bet everything on number three!
Hurry up! Smurf your bets! The race will start soon!
That's it! All betting is closed! HERE GOES!
SMURF THE LETTUCE!
YIPPEEEE! They're off!
Faster! Faster!
LET'S GO! GO, NUMBER FOUR!
?
!
What?! You, Smurfette?! You're smurfing bets too?
Uh... Not at all! I'm just here to make sure the snails aren't mistreated!
Much, much later...
Number four wins!
Z Z Z Z Z Z
Z
Uh, hey... The race is over!
Z
© Peyo

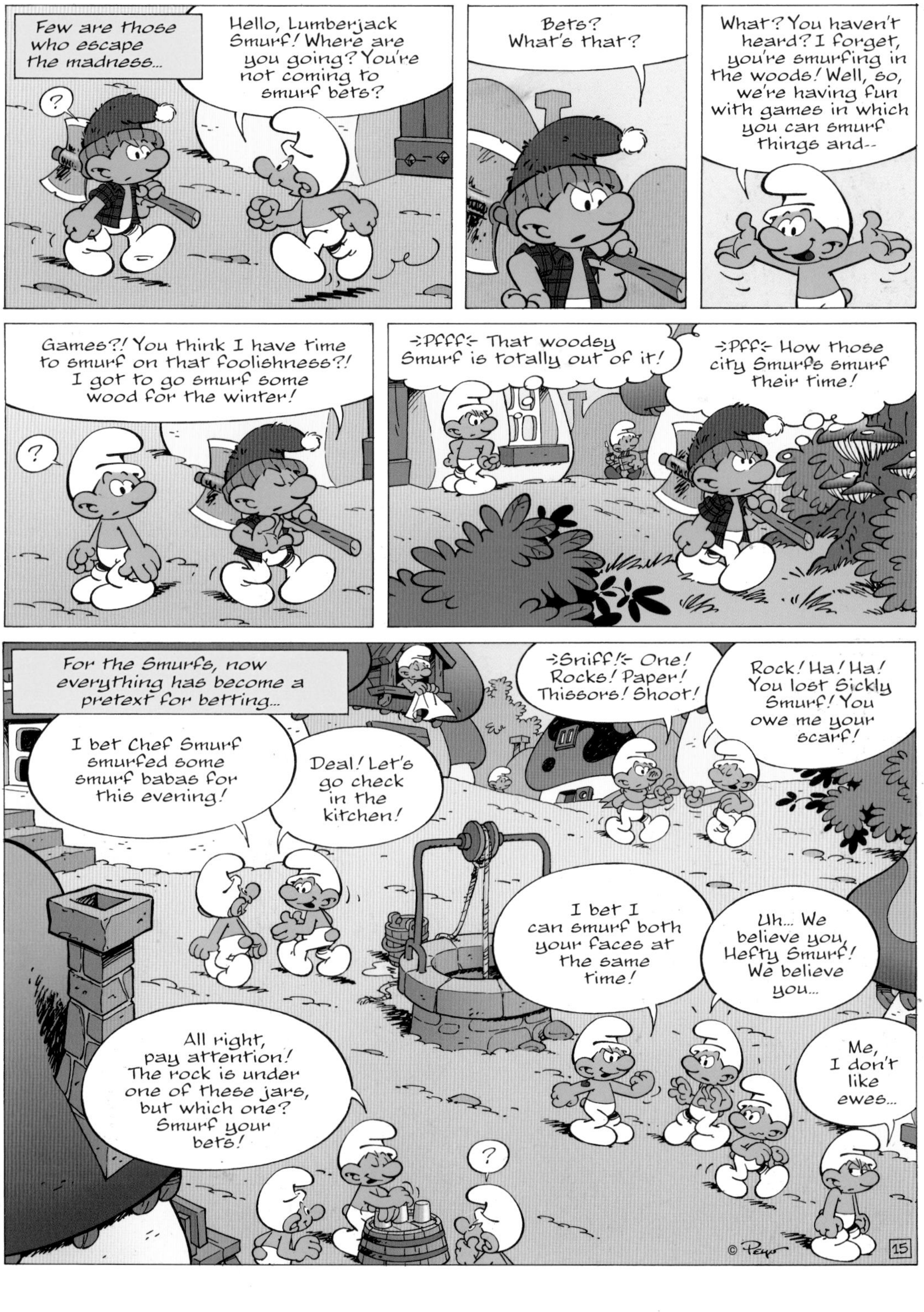

Few are those who escape the madness...
?
Hello, Lumberjack Smurf! Where are you going? You're not coming to smurf bets?
Bets? What's that?
What? You haven't heard? I forget, you're smurfing in the woods! Well, so, we're having fun with games in which you can smurf things and--
Games?! You think I have time to smurf on that foolishness?! I got to go smurf some wood for the winter!
?
-Pfff- That woodsy Smurf is totally out of it!
-Pff- How those city Smurfs smurf their time!
For the Smurfs, now everything has become a pretext for betting...
I bet Chef Smurf smurfed some smurf babas for this evening!
Deal! Let's go check in the kitchen!
-Sniff!- One! Rocks! Paper! Thissors! Shoot!
Rock! Ha! Ha! You lost Sickly Smurf! You owe me your scarf!
I bet I can smurf both your faces at the same time!
Uh... We believe you, Hefty Smurf! We believe you...
All right, pay attention! The rock is under one of these jars, but which one? Smurf your bets!
?
Me, I don't like ewes...
© Peyo
15

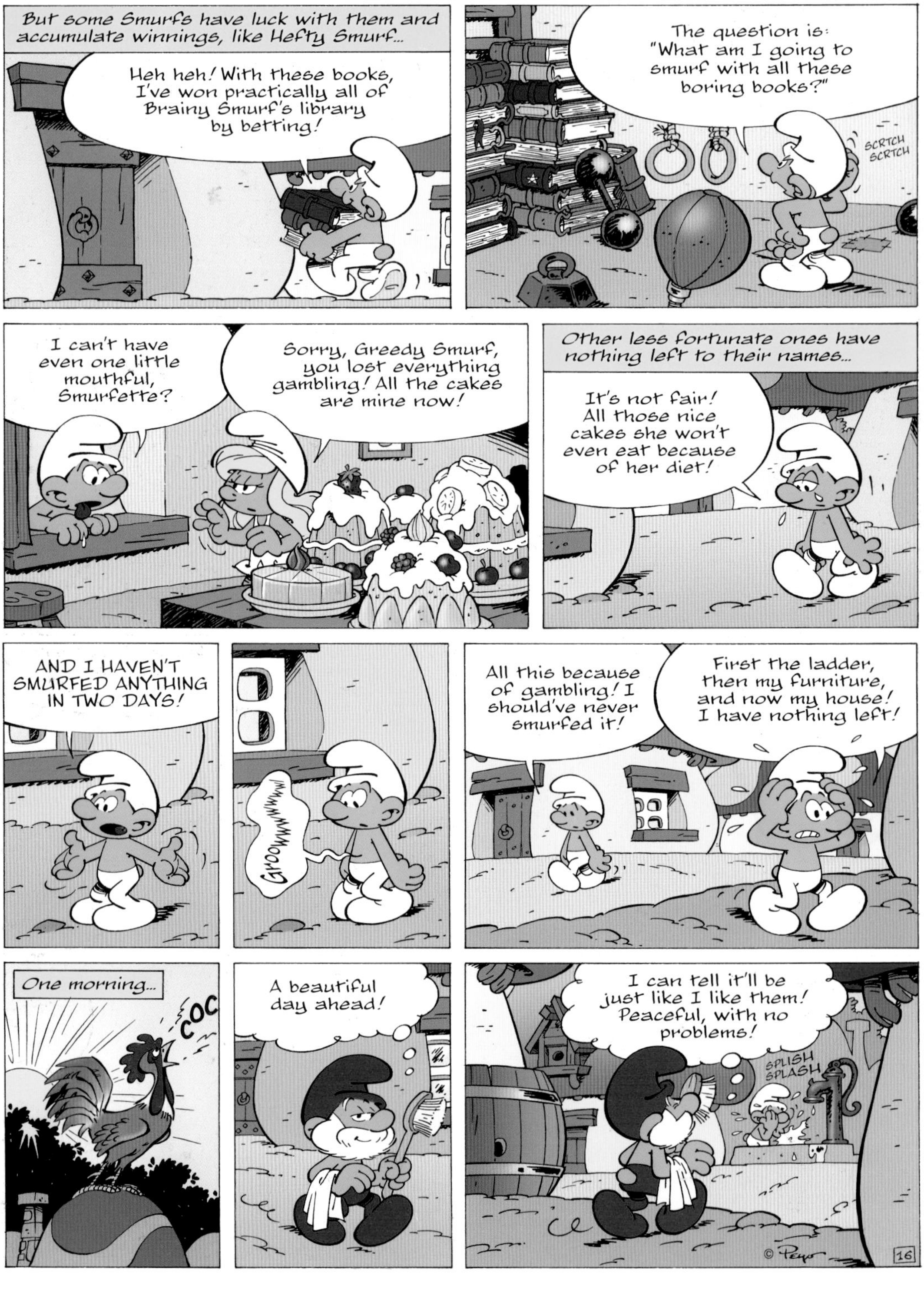
But some Smurfs have luck with them and accumulate winnings, like Hefty Smurf...
Heh heh! With these books, I've won practically all of Brainy Smurf's library by betting!
The question is: "What am I going to smurf with all these boring books?"
SCRTCH SCRTCH
I can't have even one little mouthful, Smurfette?
Sorry, Greedy Smurf, you lost everything gambling! All the cakes are mine now!
Other less fortunate ones have nothing left to their names...
It's not fair! All those nice cakes she won't even eat because of her diet!
AND I HAVEN'T SMURFED ANYTHING IN TWO DAYS!
GROOWWWWWWWW
All this because of gambling! I should've never smurfed it!
First the ladder, then my furniture, and now my house! I have nothing left!
One morning...
COC
A beautiful day ahead!
I can tell it'll be just like I like them! Peaceful, with no problems!
SPLISH SPLASH
© Peyo
16

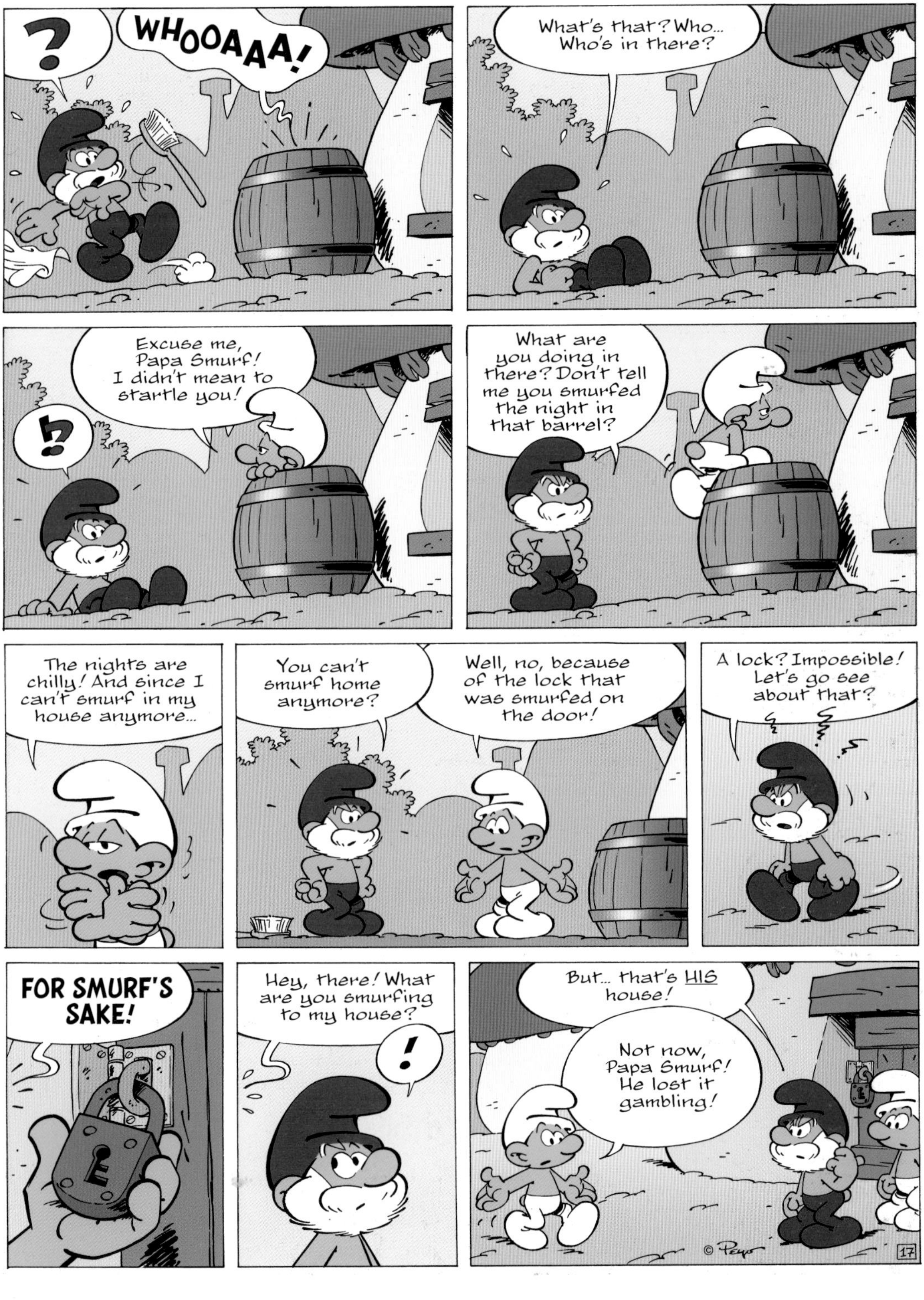
?
WHOOAAA!
What's that? Who...
Who's in there?
Excuse me, Papa Smurf! I didn't mean to startle you!
!?
What are you doing in there? Don't tell me you smurfed the night in that barrel?
The nights are chilly! And since I can't smurf in my house anymore...
You can't smurf home anymore?
Well, no, because of the lock that was smurfed on the door!
A lock? Impossible! Let's go see about that?
FOR SMURF'S SAKE!
Hey, there! What are you smurfing to my house?
!
But... that's HIS house!
Not now, Papa Smurf! He lost it gambling!
© Peyo
17

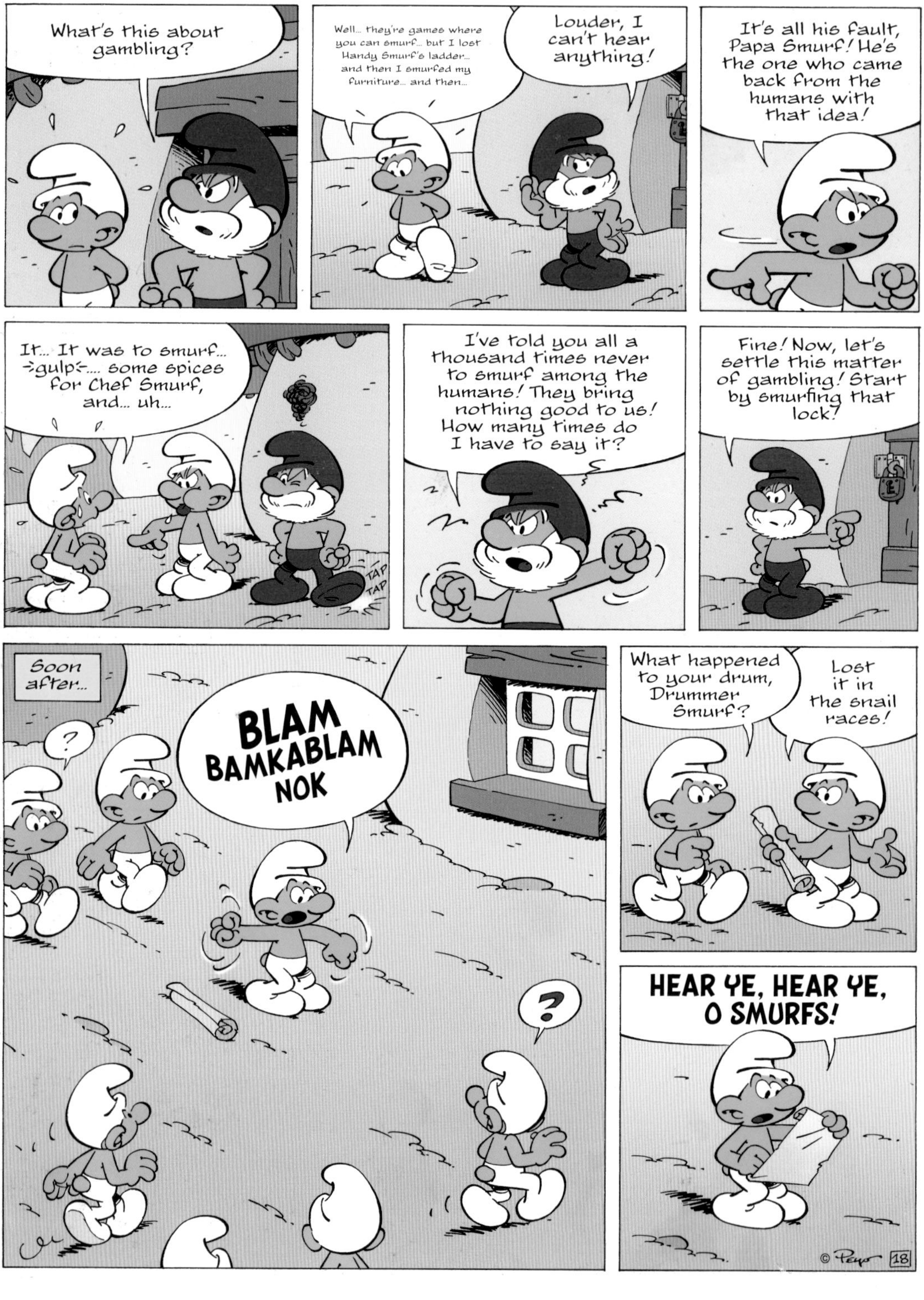
What's this about gambling?
Well... they're games where you can smurf... but I lost Handy Smurf's ladder... and then I smurfed my furniture... and then...
Louder, I can't hear anything!
It's all his fault, Papa Smurf! He's the one who came back from the humans with that idea!
It... It was to smurf... -gulp-... some spices for Chef Smurf, and... uh...
TAP TAP
I've told you all a thousand times never to smurf among the humans! They bring nothing good to us! How many times do I have to say it?
Fine! Now, let's settle this matter of gambling! Start by smurfing that lock!
Soon after...
?
BLAM BAMKABLAM NOK
?
What happened to your drum, Drummer Smurf?
Lost it in the snail races!
HEAR YE, HEAR YE, O SMURFS!
© Peyo
18

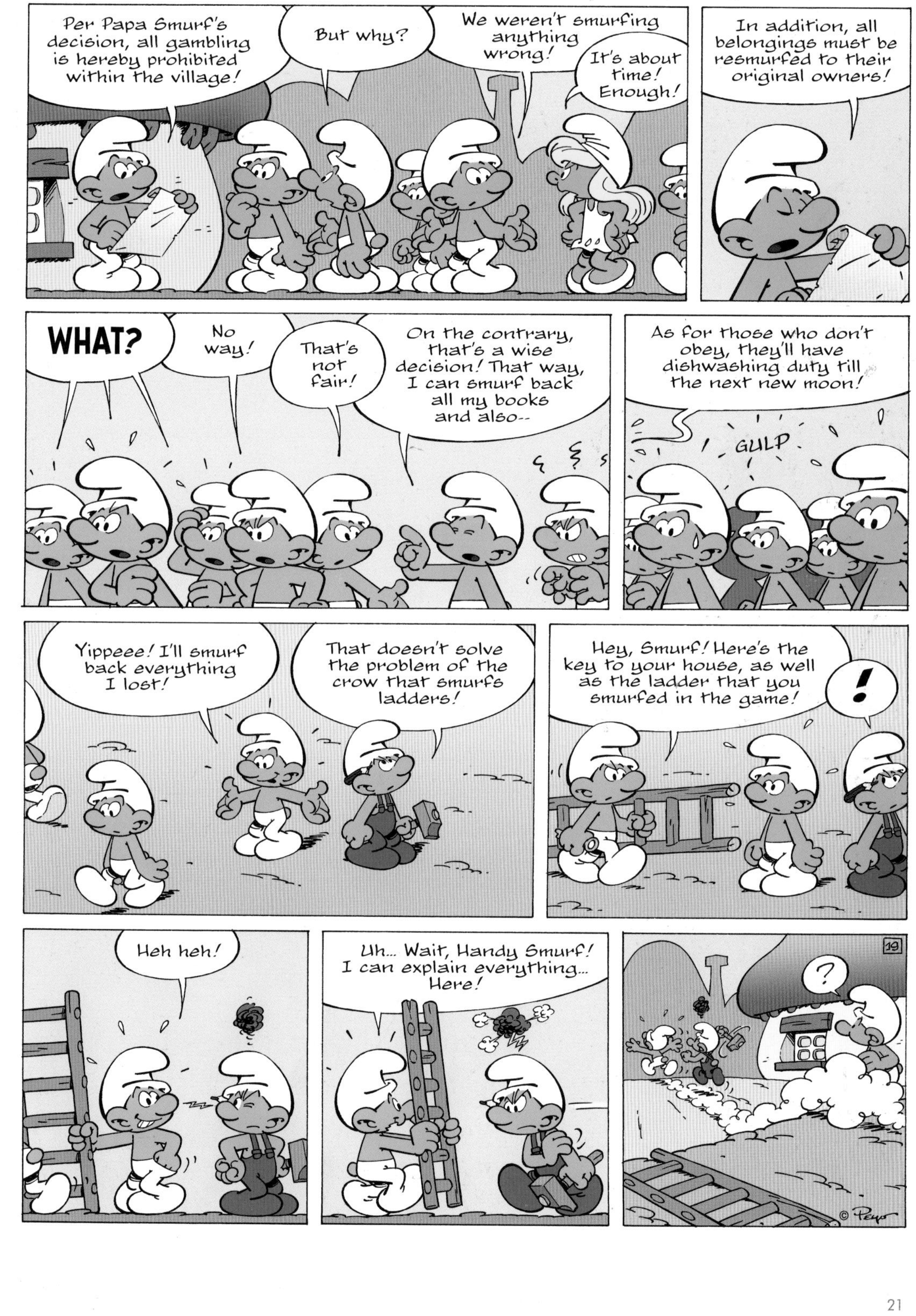
Per Papa Smurf's decision, all gambling is hereby prohibited within the village!
But why?
We weren't smurfing anything wrong!
It's about time! Enough!
In addition, all belongings must be resmurfed to their original owners!
WHAT?
No way!
That's not fair!
On the contrary, that's a wise decision! That way, I can smurf back all my books and also--
As for those who don't obey, they'll have dishwashing duty till the next new moon!
GULP
Yippeee! I'll smurf back everything I lost!
That doesn't solve the problem of the crow that smurfs ladders!
Hey, Smurf! Here's the key to your house, as well as the ladder that you smurfed in the game!
!
Heh heh!
Uh... Wait, Handy Smurf! I can explain everything... Here!
19
?
© Peyo

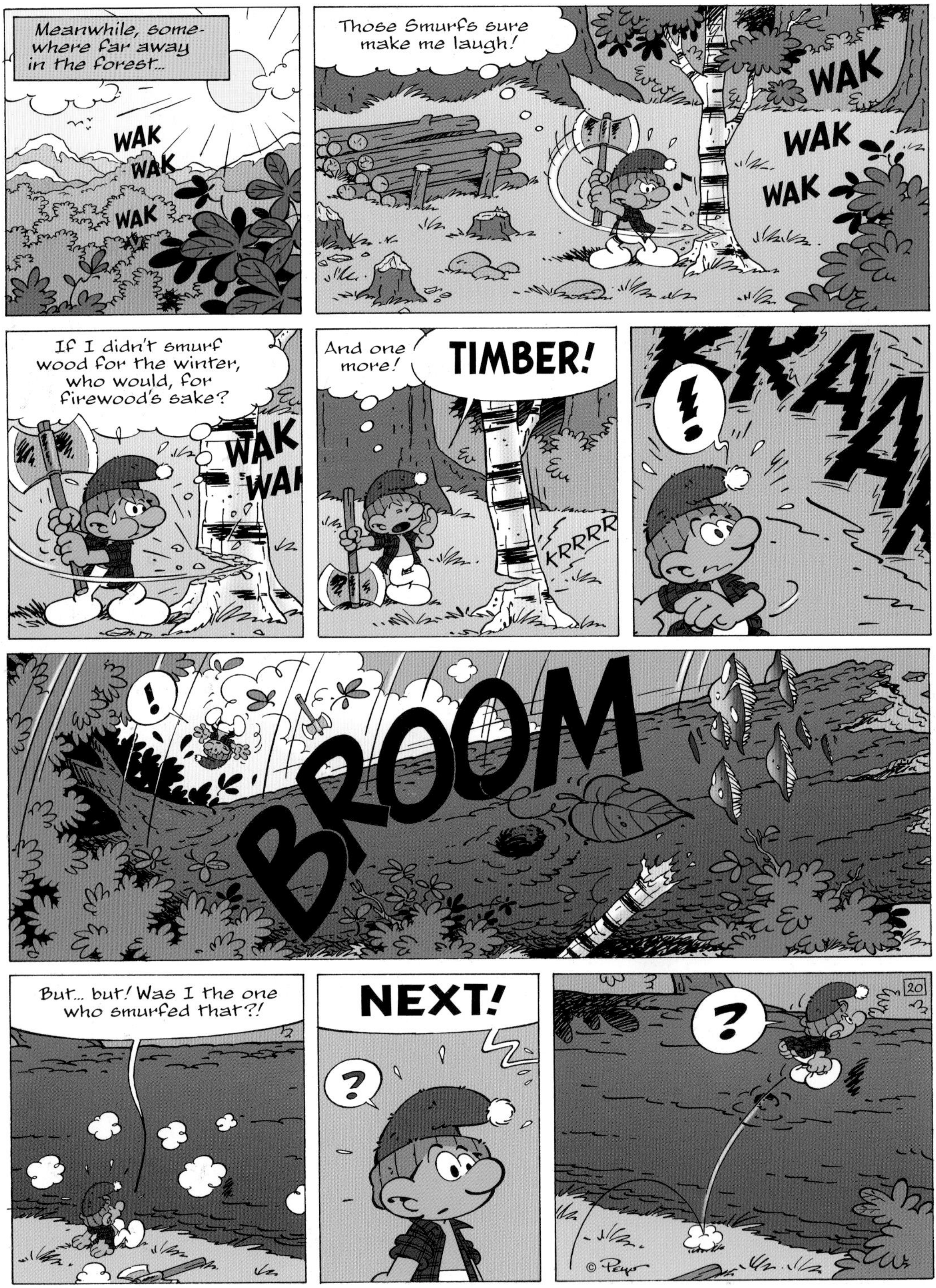
Meanwhile, somewhere far away in the forest...
WAK
WAK
WAK
Those Smurfs sure make me laugh!
WAK
WAK
WAK
If I didn't smurf wood for the winter, who would, for firewood's sake?
WAK
WAK
And one more!
TIMBER!
KRRRR
!
BROOM
!
But... but! Was I the one who smurfed that?!
NEXT!
?
?
© Peyo

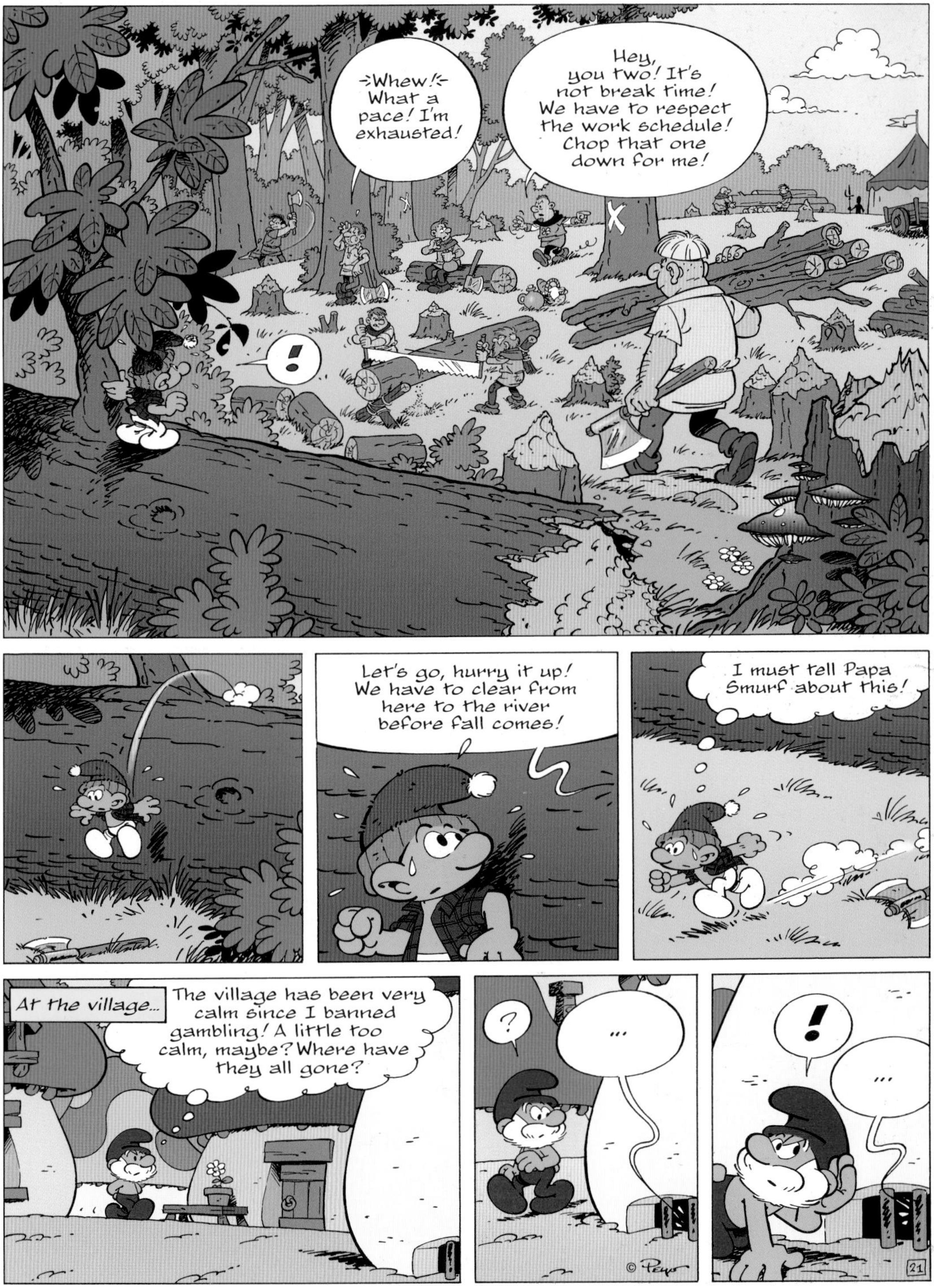

Whew! What a pace! I'm exhausted!
Hey, you two! It's not break time! We have to respect the work schedule! Chop that one down for me!
!
Let's go, hurry it up! We have to clear from here to the river before fall comes!
I must tell Papa Smurf about this!
At the village...
The village has been very calm since I banned gambling! A little too calm, maybe? Where have they all gone?
?
...
!
...
© Peyo
21

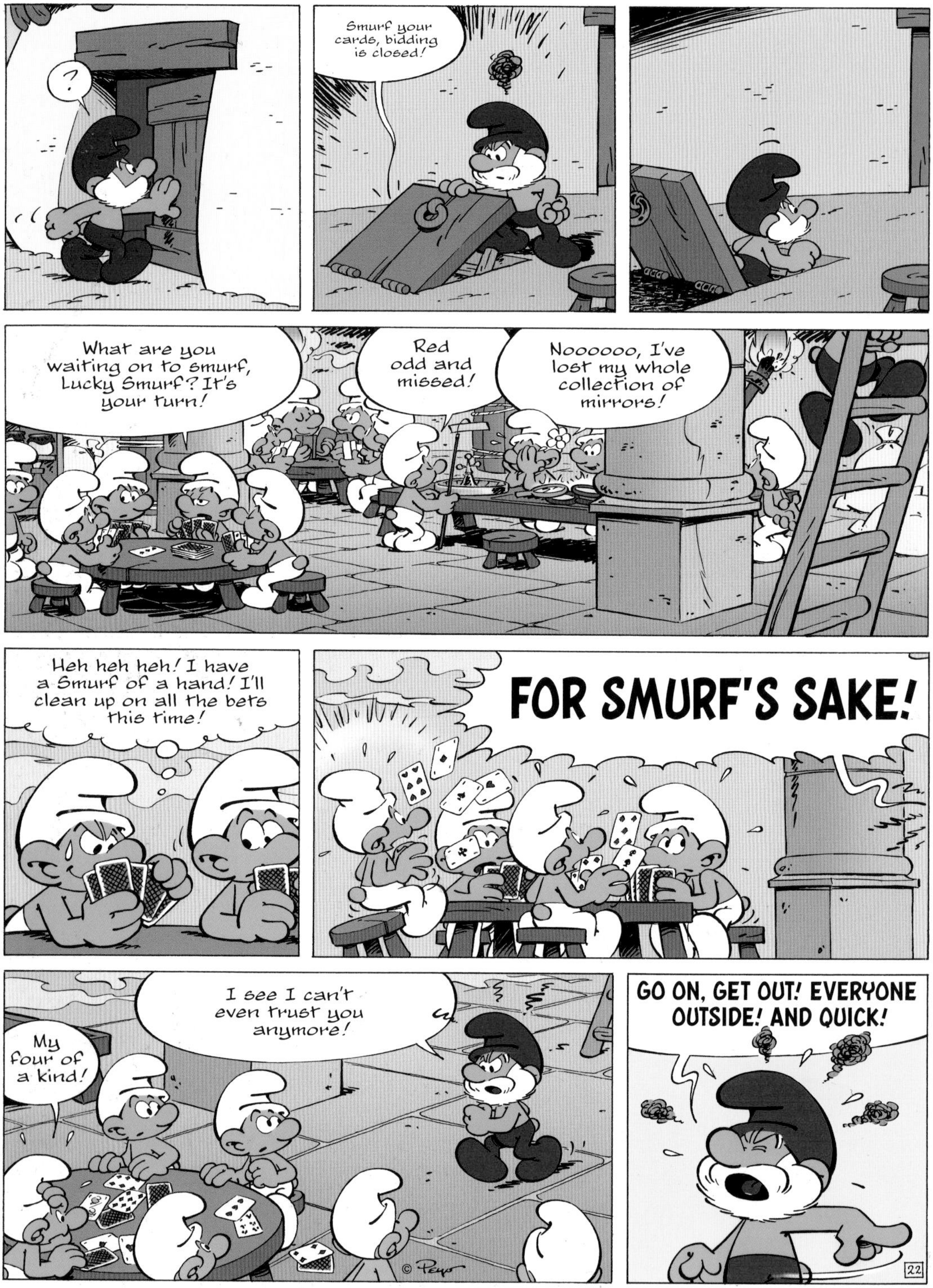
?
Smurf your cards, bidding is closed!
What are you waiting on to smurf, Lucky Smurf? It's your turn!
Red odd and missed!
Noooooo, I've lost my whole collection of mirrors!
Heh heh heh! I have a Smurf of a hand! I'll clean up on all the bets this time!
FOR SMURF'S SAKE!
My four of a kind!
I see I can't even trust you anymore!
GO ON, GET OUT! EVERYONE OUTSIDE! AND QUICK!
© Peyo
22

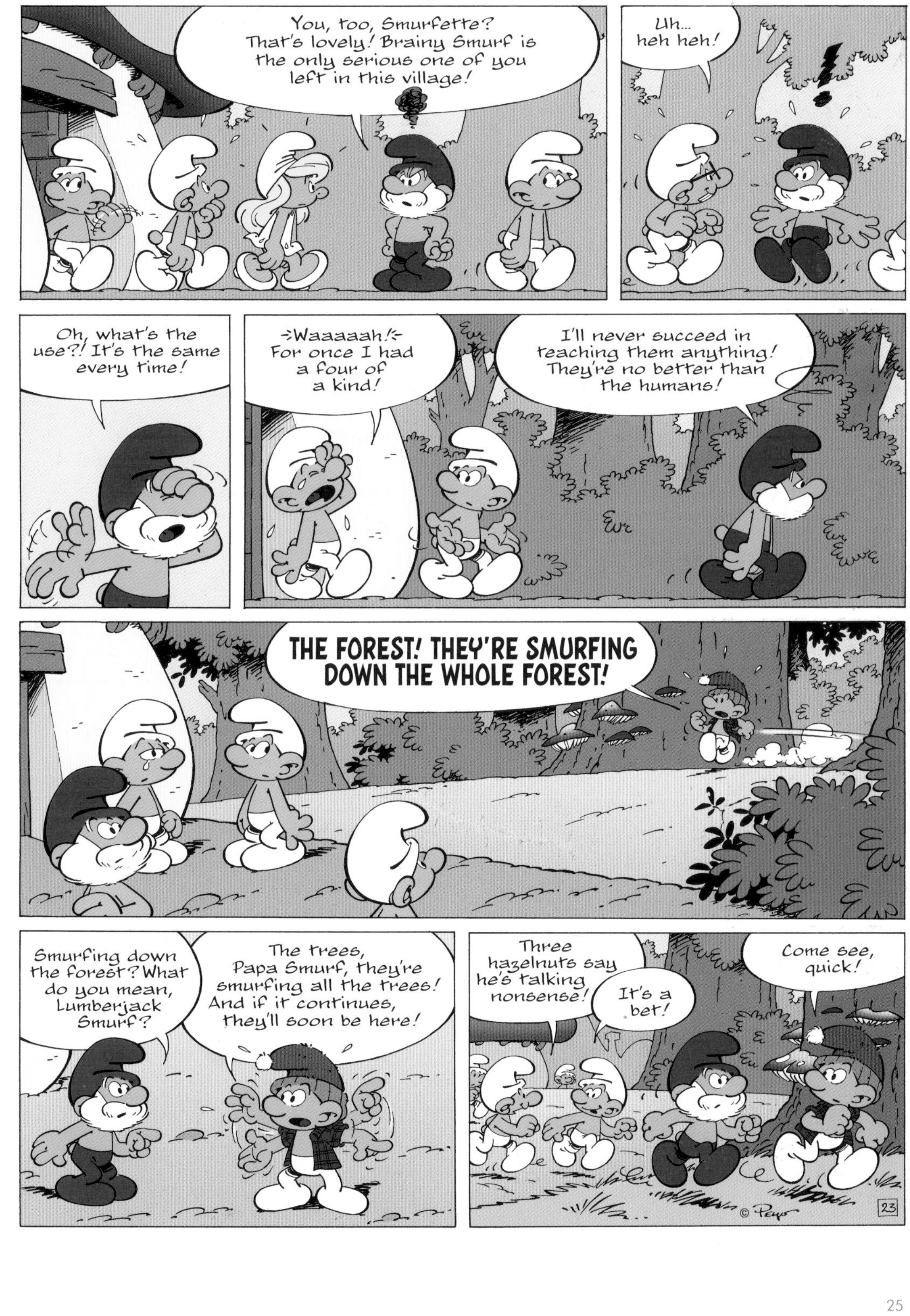
You, too, Smurfette? That's lovely! Brainy Smurf is the only serious one of you left in this village!
Uh... heh heh!
Oh, what's the use?! It's the same every time!
-Waaaaah!- For once I had a four of a kind!
I'll never succeed in teaching them anything! They're no better than the humans!
THE FOREST! THEY'RE SMURFING DOWN THE WHOLE FOREST!
Smurfing down the forest? What do you mean, Lumberjack Smurf?
The trees, Papa Smurf, they're smurfing all the trees! And if it continues, they'll soon be here!
Three hazelnuts say he's talking nonsense!
It's a bet!
Come see, quick!
23
© Peyo

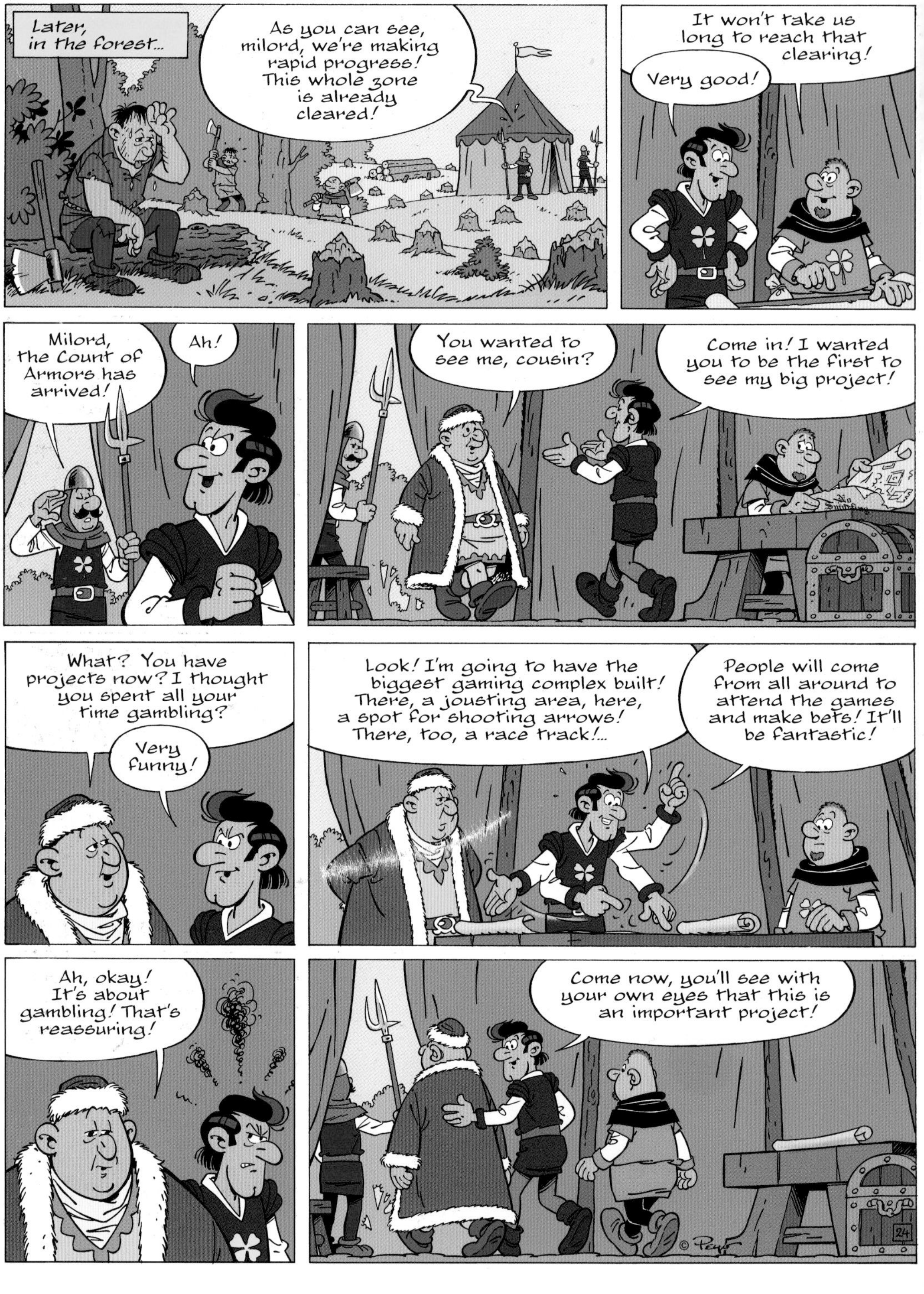
Later, in the forest...
As you can see, milord, we're making rapid progress! This whole zone is already cleared!
It won't take us long to reach that clearing!
Very good!
Milord, the Count of Armors has arrived!
Ah!
You wanted to see me, cousin?
Come in! I wanted you to be the first to see my big project!
What? You have projects now? I thought you spent all your time gambling?
Very funny!
Look! I'm going to have the biggest gaming complex built! There, a jousting area, here, a spot for shooting arrows! There, too, a race track!...
People will come from all around to attend the games and make bets! It'll be fantastic!
Ah, okay! It's about gambling! That's reassuring!
Come now, you'll see with your own eyes that this is an important project!
© Peyo
24

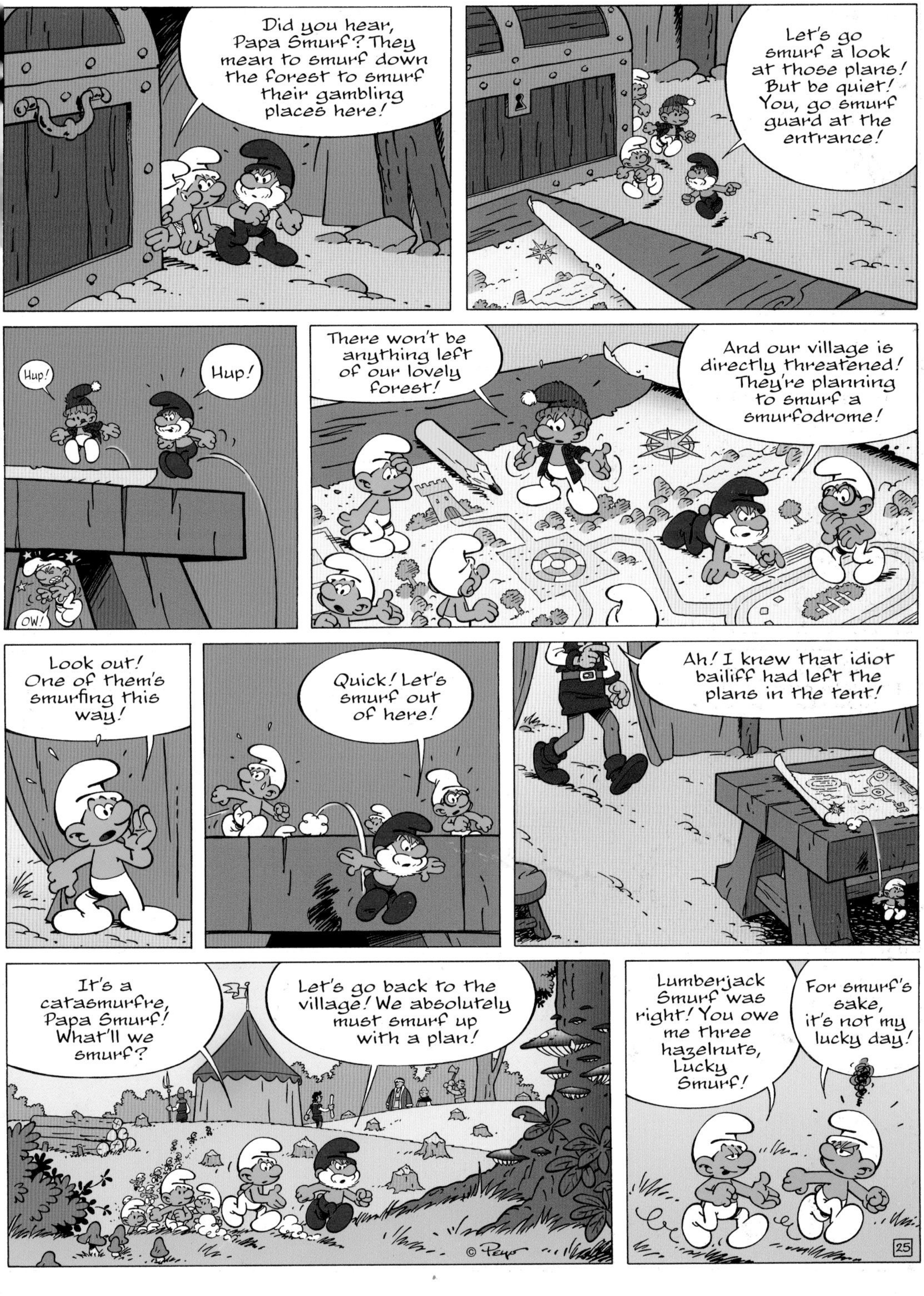

Did you hear, Papa Smurf? They mean to smurf down the forest to smurf their gambling places here!
Let's go smurf a look at those plans! But be quiet! You, go smurf guard at the entrance!
Hup!
Hup!
OW!
There won't be anything left of our lovely forest!
And our village is directly threatened! They're planning to smurf a smurfodrome!
Look out! One of them's smurfing this way!
Quick! Let's smurf out of here!
Ah! I knew that idiot bailiff had left the plans in the tent!
It's a catasmurfre, Papa Smurf! What'll we smurf?
Let's go back to the village! We absolutely must smurf up with a plan!
© Peyo
Lumberjack Smurf was right! You owe me three hazelnuts, Lucky Smurf!
For smurf's sake, it's not my lucky day!
25

What comforts me is that Gargamel's shack will be smurfed too!

That's true! I saw that on the plans too!

Hmm! Maybe... Why not? It's risky, but it's our only chance!

What is it, Papa Smurf?

Three hazelnuts says he comes up with a solution!

It's a bet!

SMACK

Follow me, I think I've smurfed a solution!

?

?

I must get revenge on those cursed Smurfs!

They pulled a good one on me that last time with that story of an imaginary illness!*

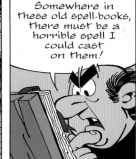

Somewhere in these old spell-books, there must be a horrible spell I could cast on them!

?

NOK NOK

Who could that be?

THE SMURFS!

© Peyo

26

* See: THE SMURFS #24 "The Smurf Reporter."

28

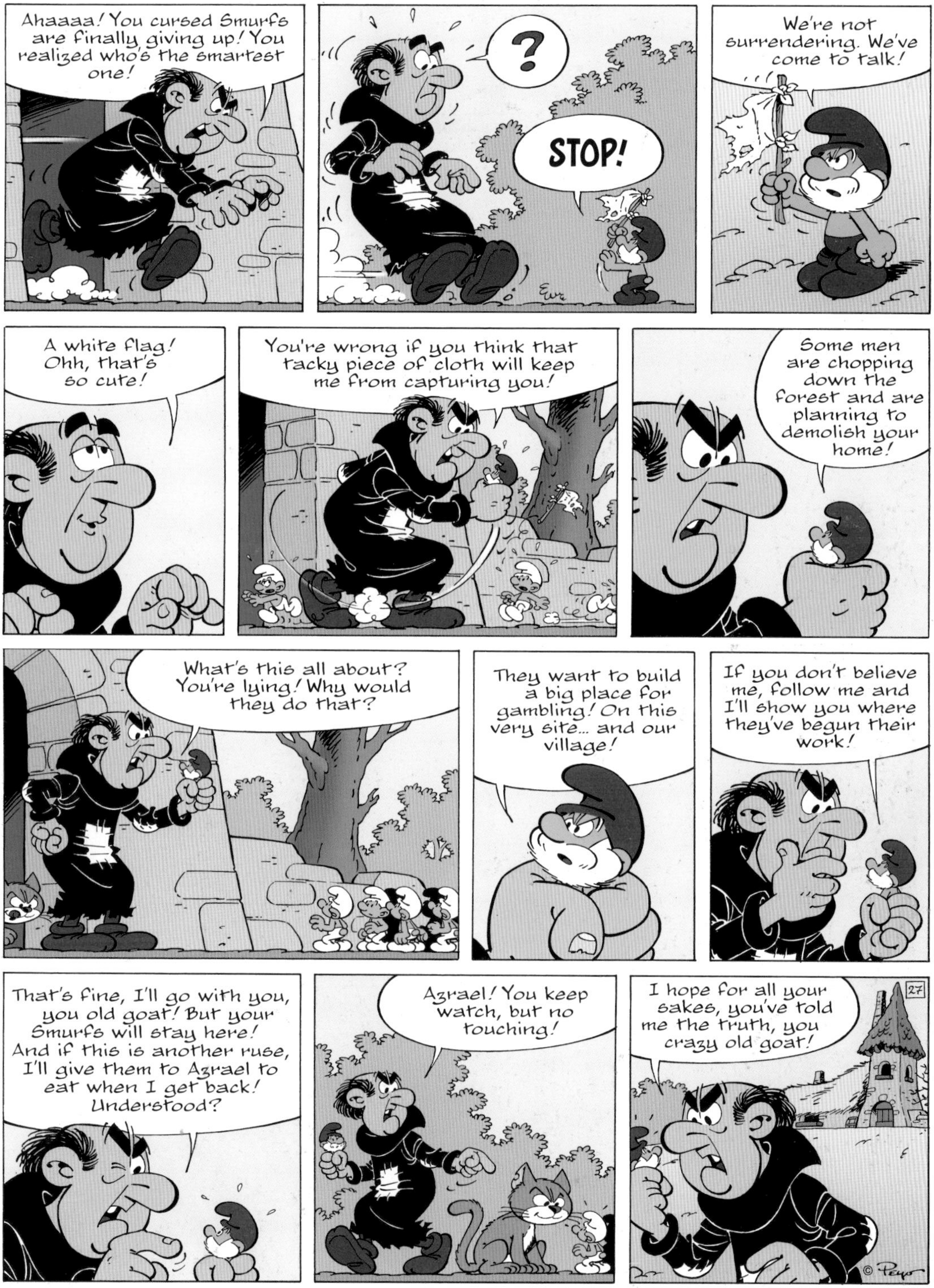

Ahaaaa! You cursed Smurfs are finally giving up! You realized who's the smartest one!
?
STOP!
We're not surrendering. We've come to talk!
A white flag! Ohh, that's so cute!
You're wrong if you think that tacky piece of cloth will keep me from capturing you!
Some men are chopping down the forest and are planning to demolish your home!
What's this all about? You're lying! Why would they do that?
They want to build a big place for gambling! On this very site... and our village!
If you don't believe me, follow me and I'll show you where they've begun their work!
That's fine, I'll go with you, you old goat! But your Smurfs will stay here! And if this is another ruse, I'll give them to Azrael to eat when I get back! Understood?
Azrael! You keep watch, but no touching!
I hope for all your sakes, you've told me the truth, you crazy old goat!
27
© Peyo

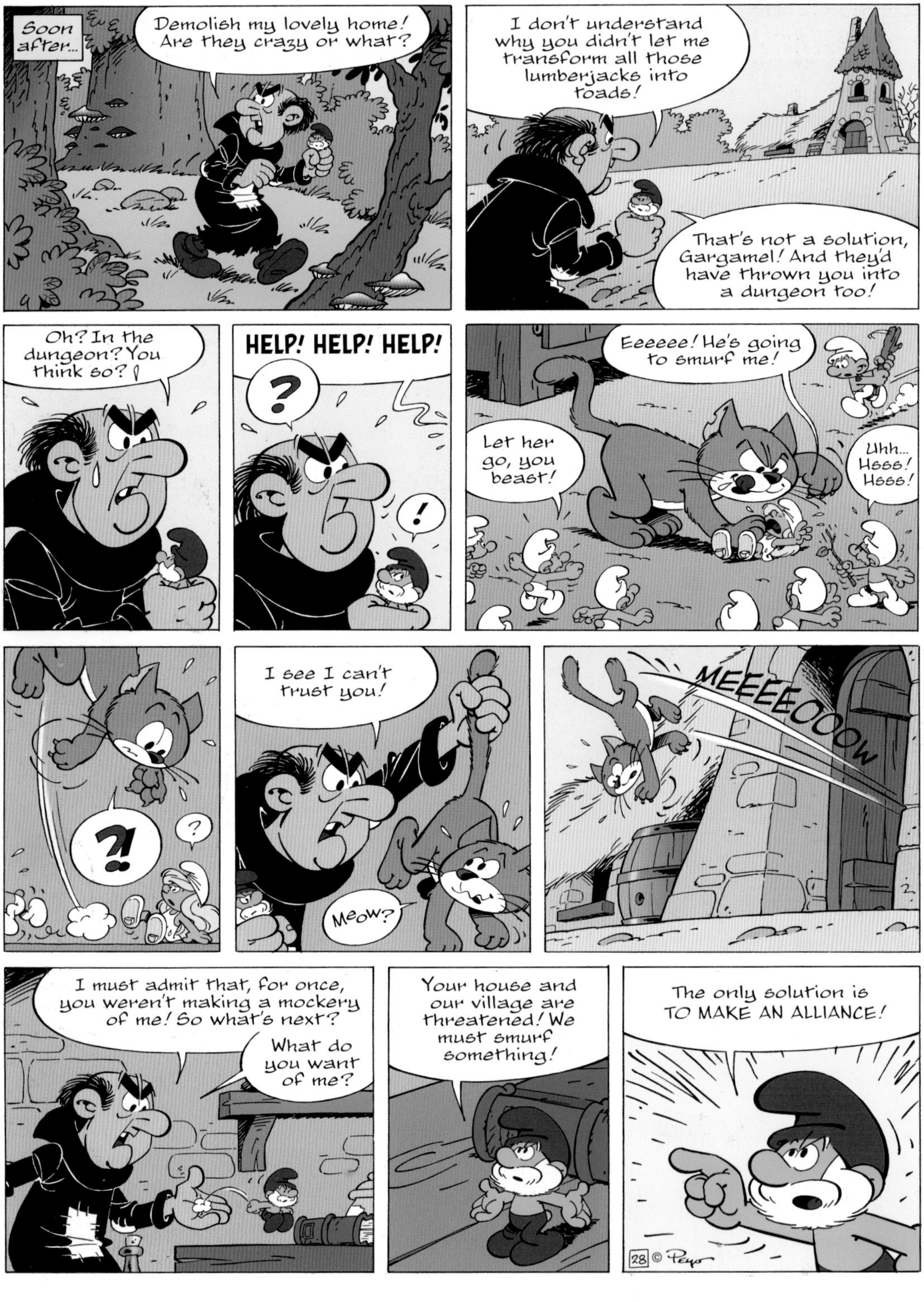

Soon after...
Demolish my lovely home! Are they crazy or what?
I don't understand why you didn't let me transform all those lumberjacks into toads!
That's not a solution, Gargamel! And they'd have thrown you into a dungeon too!
Oh? In the dungeon? You think so?
HELP! HELP! HELP!
?
!
Eeeeee! He's going to smurf me!
Let her go, you beast!
Uhh... Hsss! Hsss!
?!
?
I see I can't trust you!
Meow?
MEEEEOOOOW
I must admit that, for once, you weren't making a mockery of me! So what's next?
What do you want of me?
Your house and our village are threatened! We must smurf something!
The only solution is TO MAKE AN ALLIANCE!
28 © Peyo

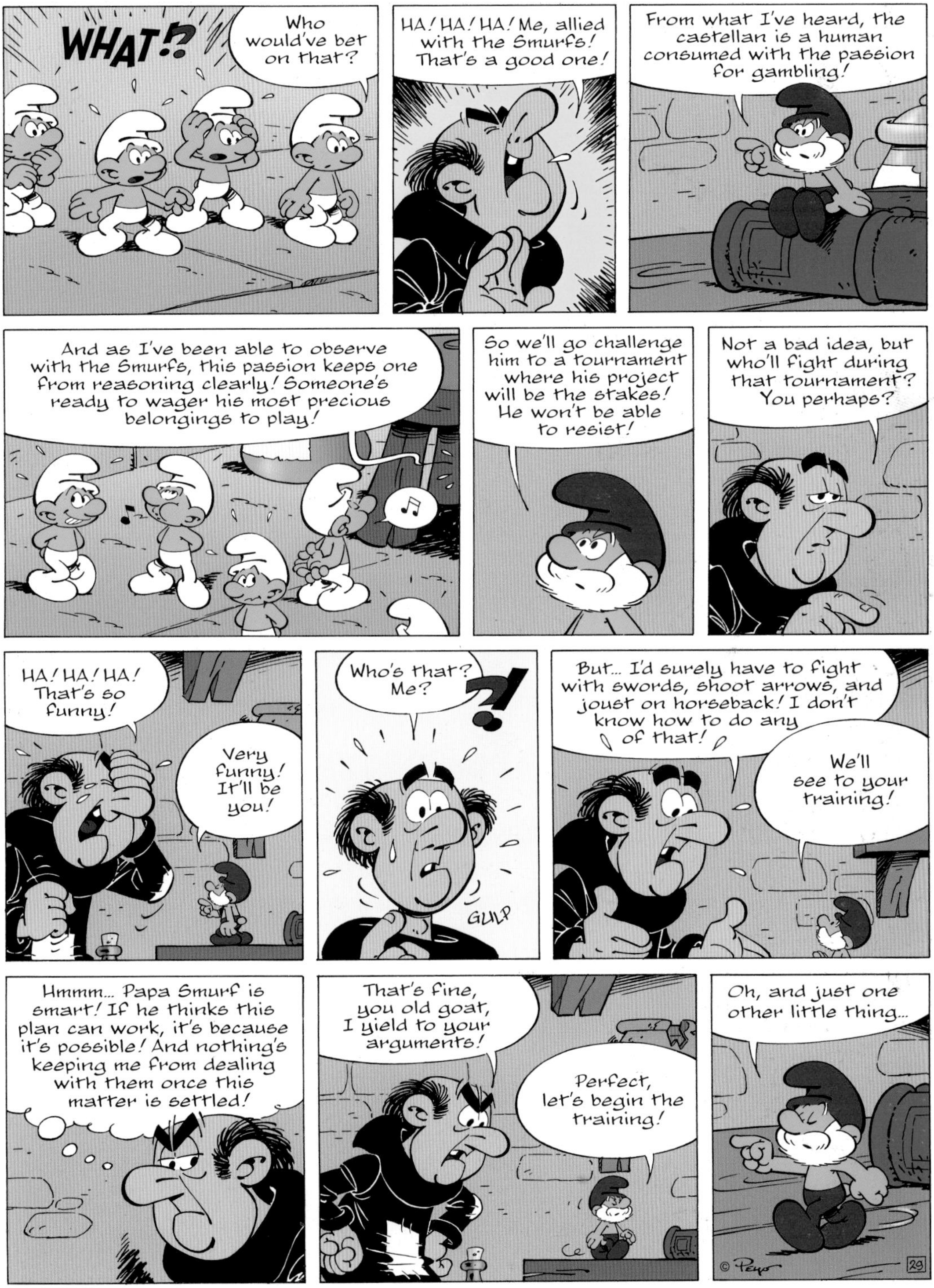
WHAT!?
Who would've bet on that?
HA! HA! HA! Me, allied with the Smurfs! That's a good one!
From what I've heard, the castellan is a human consumed with the passion for gambling!
And as I've been able to observe with the Smurfs, this passion keeps one from reasoning clearly! Someone's ready to wager his most precious belongings to play!
So we'll go challenge him to a tournament where his project will be the stakes! He won't be able to resist!
Not a bad idea, but who'll fight during that tournament? You perhaps?
HA! HA! HA! That's so funny!
Very funny! It'll be you!
Who's that? Me?
GULP
But... I'd surely have to fight with swords, shoot arrows, and joust on horseback! I don't know how to do any of that!
We'll see to your training!
Hmmm... Papa Smurf is smart! If he thinks this plan can work, it's because it's possible! And nothing's keeping me from dealing with them once this matter is settled!
That's fine, you old goat, I yield to your arguments!
Perfect, let's begin the training!
Oh, and just one other little thing...
© Peyo
29

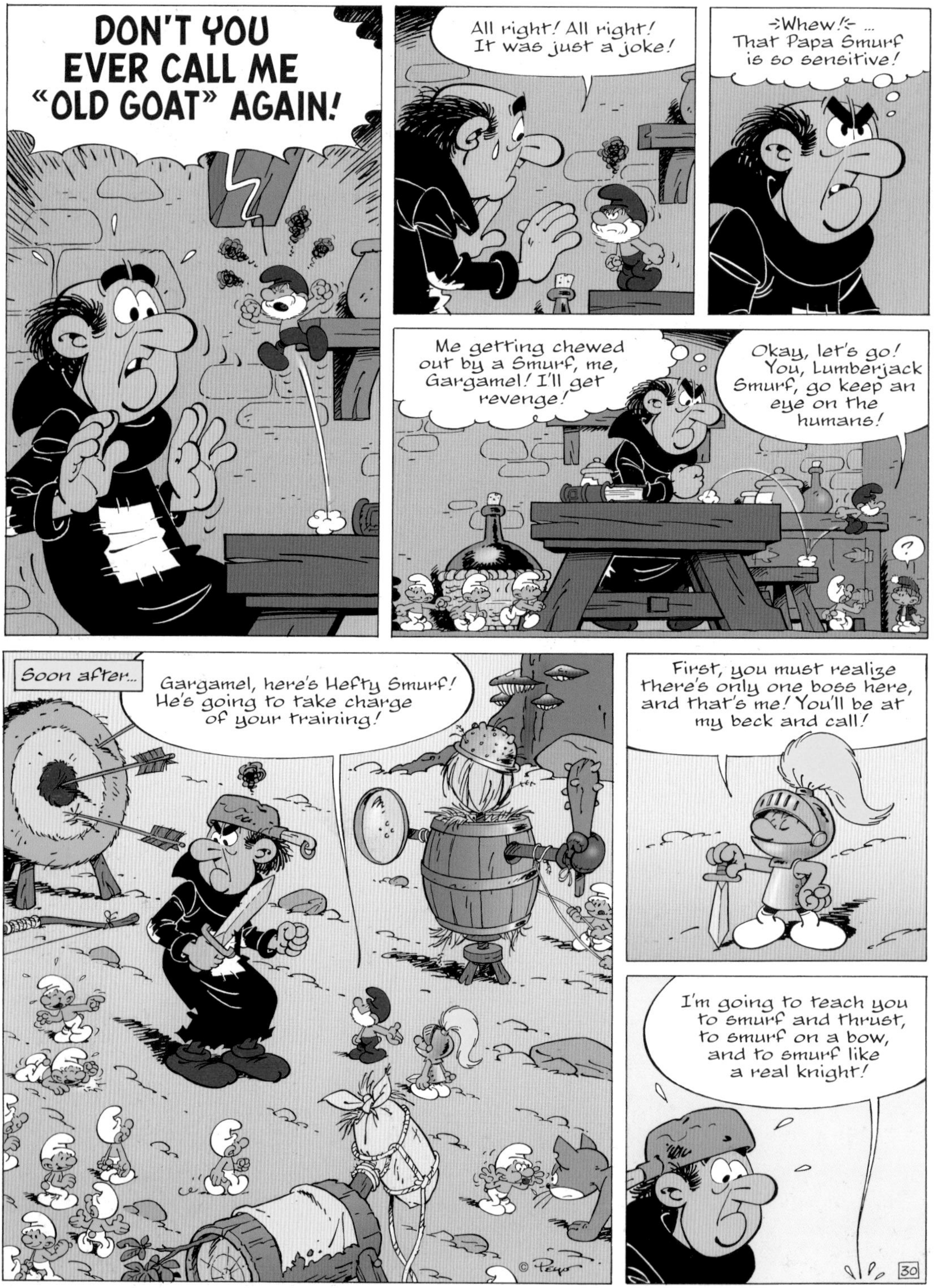

DON'T YOU EVER CALL ME «OLD GOAT» AGAIN!
All right! All right! It was just a joke!
Whew! ... That Papa Smurf is so sensitive!
Me getting chewed out by a Smurf, me, Gargamel! I'll get revenge!
Okay, let's go! You, Lumberjack Smurf, go keep an eye on the humans!
?
Soon after...
Gargamel, here's Hefty Smurf! He's going to take charge of your training!
First, you must realize there's only one boss here, and that's me! You'll be at my beck and call!
I'm going to teach you to smurf and thrust, to smurf on a bow, and to smurf like a real knight!
© Peyo
30

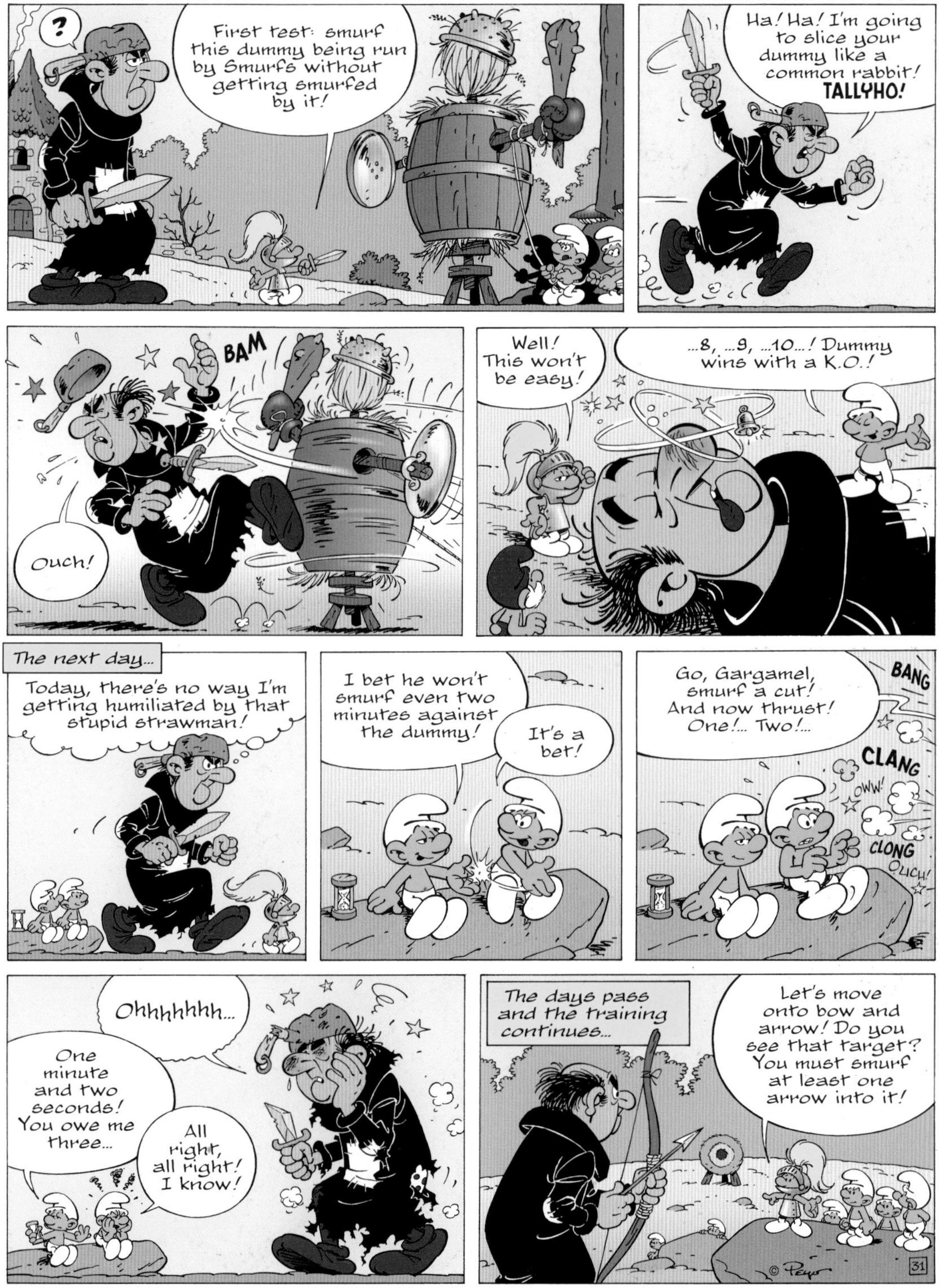
?
First test: smurf this dummy being run by Smurfs without getting smurfed by it!
Ha! Ha! I'm going to slice your dummy like a common rabbit! TALLYHO!
BAM
Ouch!
Well! This won't be easy!
...8, ...9, ...10...! Dummy wins with a K.O.!
The next day...
Today, there's no way I'm getting humiliated by that stupid strawman!
I bet he won't smurf even two minutes against the dummy!
It's a bet!
Go, Gargamel, smurf a cut! And now thrust! One!... Two!...
BANG
CLANG
OWW!
CLONG
OUCH!
Ohhhhhhh...
One minute and two seconds! You owe me three...
All right, all right! I know!
The days pass and the training continues...
Let's move onto bow and arrow! Do you see that target? You must smurf at least one arrow into it!
© Peyo
31

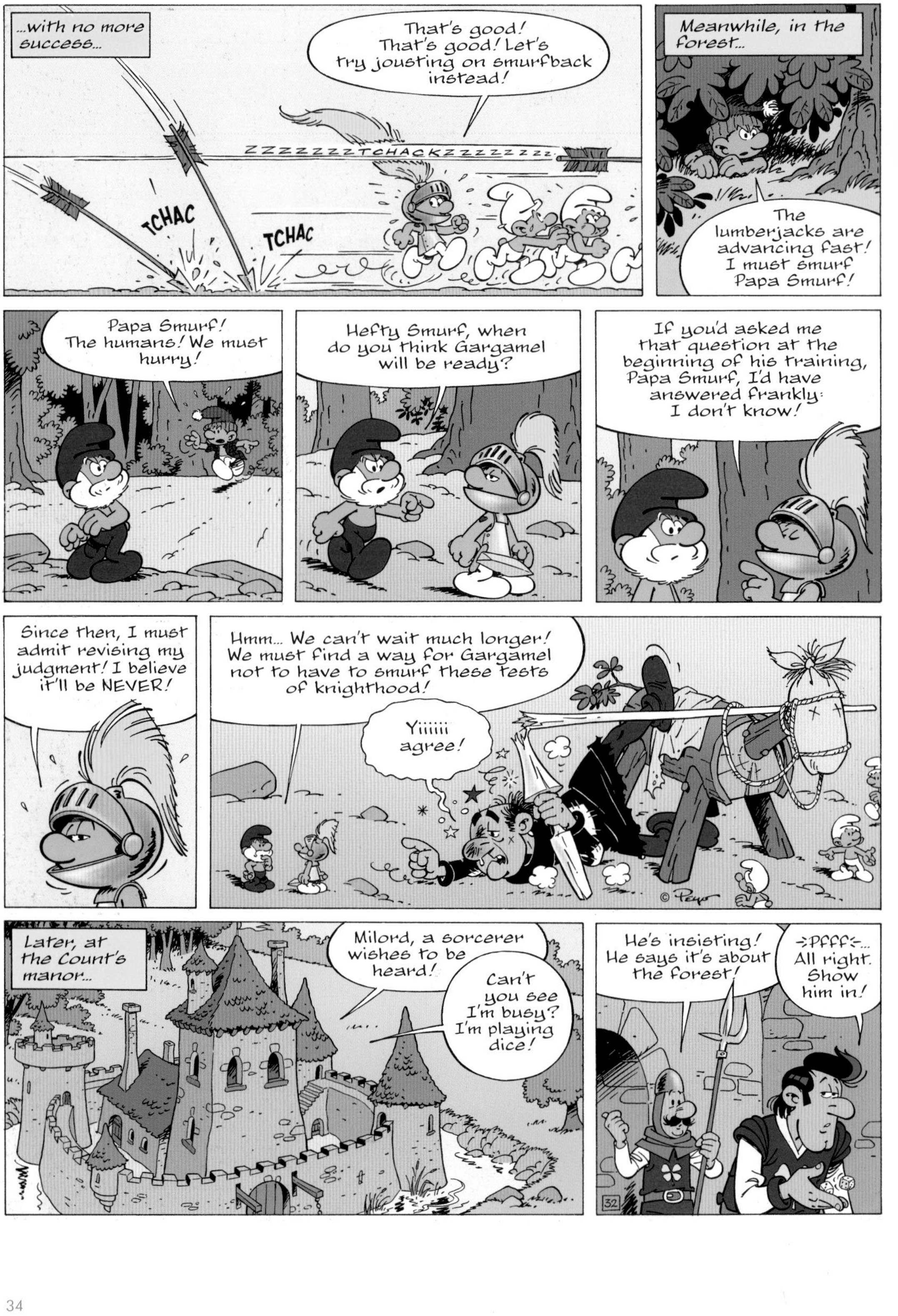
...with no more success...
That's good! That's good! Let's try jousting on smurfback instead!
ZZZZZZZTCHACKZZZZZZZZZ
TCHAC
TCHAC
Meanwhile, in the forest...
The lumberjacks are advancing fast! I must smurf Papa Smurf!
Papa Smurf! The humans! We must hurry!
Hefty Smurf, when do you think Gargamel will be ready?
If you'd asked me that question at the beginning of his training, Papa Smurf, I'd have answered frankly: I don't know!
Since then, I must admit revising my judgment! I believe it'll be NEVER!
Hmm... We can't wait much longer! We must find a way for Gargamel not to have to smurf these tests of knighthood!
Yiiiiii agree!
© Peyo
Later, at the Count's manor...
Milord, a sorcerer wishes to be heard!
Can't you see I'm busy? I'm playing dice!
He's insisting! He says it's about the forest!
-Pfff-... All right. Show him in!

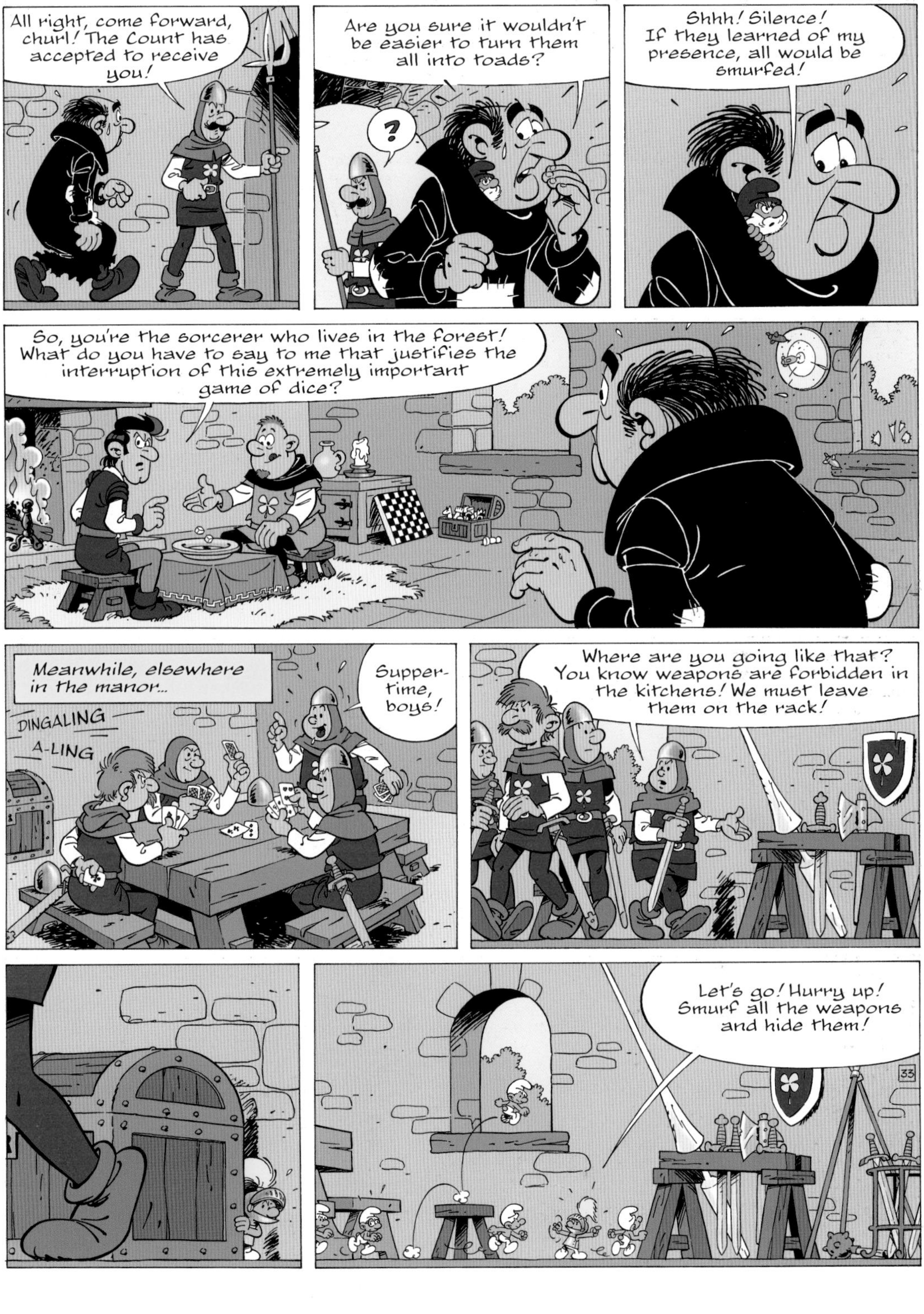
All right, come forward, churl! The Count has accepted to receive you!
Are you sure it wouldn't be easier to turn them all into toads?
?
Shhh! Silence! If they learned of my presence, all would be smurfed!
So, you're the sorcerer who lives in the forest! What do you have to say to me that justifies the interruption of this extremely important game of dice?
Meanwhile, elsewhere in the manor...
DINGALING
A-LING
Supper-time, boys!
Where are you going like that? You know weapons are forbidden in the kitchens! We must leave them on the rack!
Let's go! Hurry up! Smurf all the weapons and hide them!
33

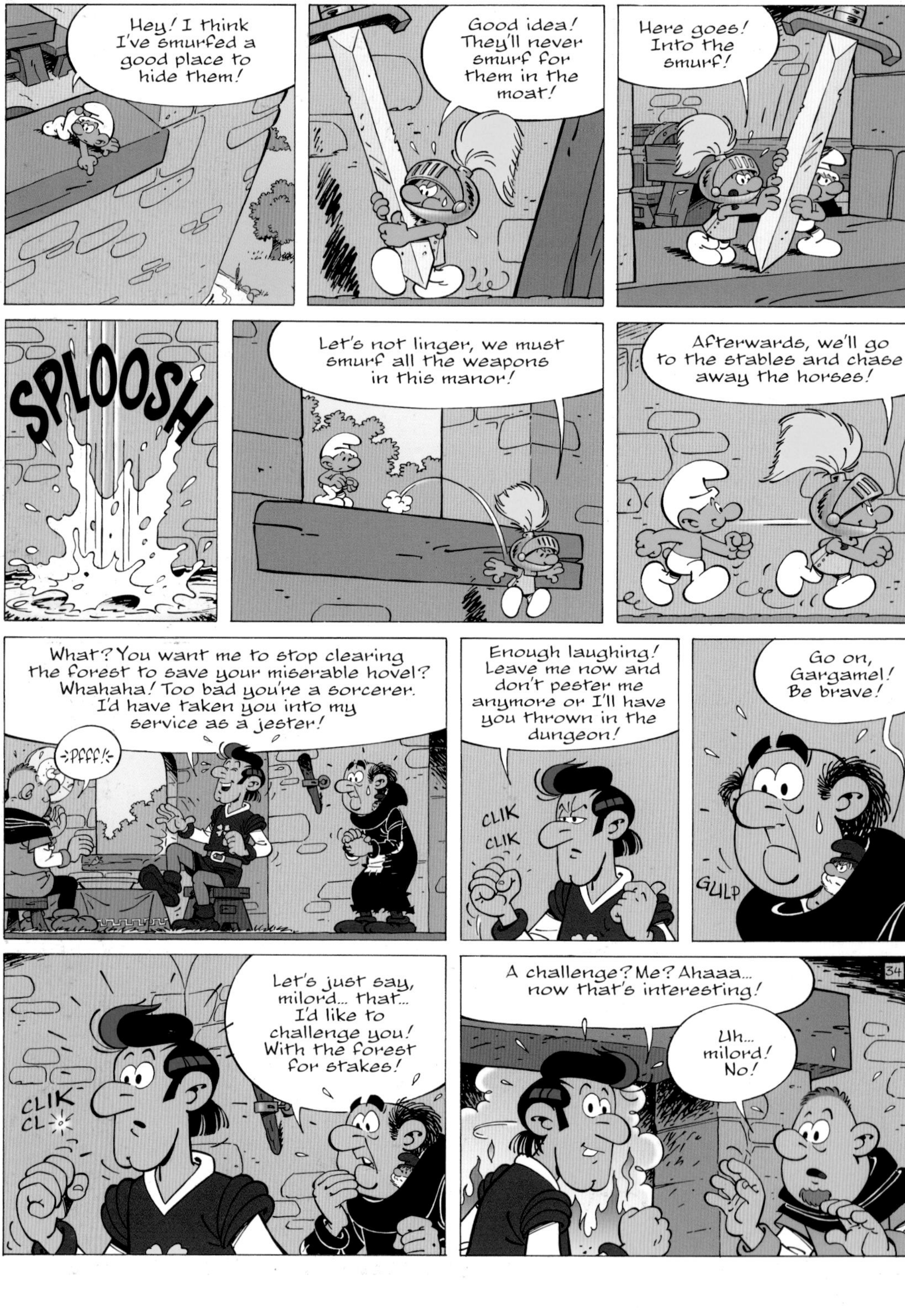

Hey! I think I've smurfed a good place to hide them!
Good idea! They'll never smurf for them in the moat!
Here goes! Into the smurf!
SPLOOSH
Let's not linger, we must smurf all the weapons in this manor!
Afterwards, we'll go to the stables and chase away the horses!
What? You want me to stop clearing the forest to save your miserable hovel? Whahaha! Too bad you're a sorcerer. I'd have taken you into my service as a jester!
PFFF!
Enough laughing! Leave me now and don't pester me anymore or I'll have you thrown in the dungeon!
CLIK CLIK
Go on, Gargamel! Be brave!
GULP
Let's just say, milord... that... I'd like to challenge you! With the forest for stakes!
CLIK CL
A challenge? Me? Ahaaa... now that's interesting!
34
Uh... milord! No!

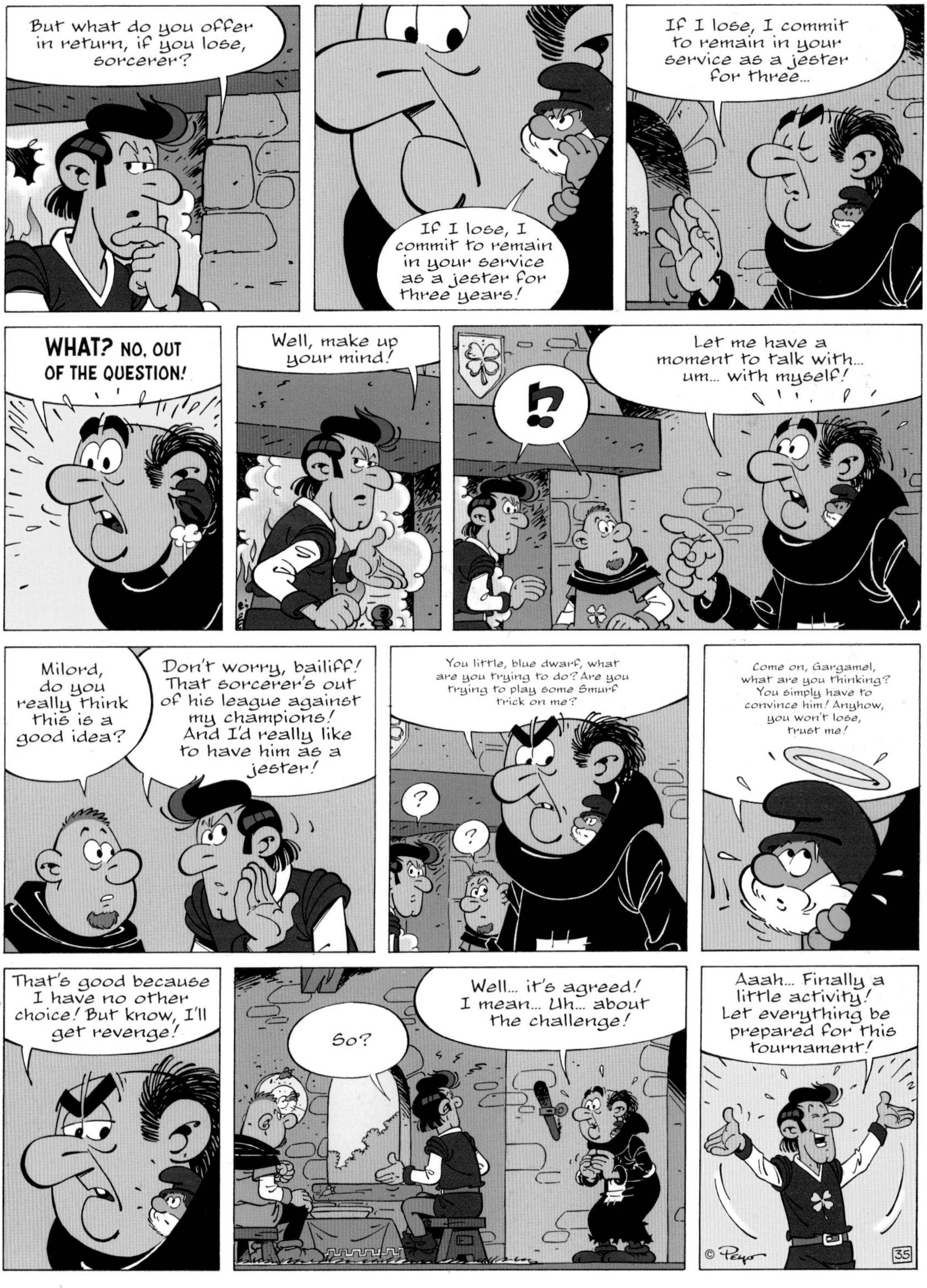
But what do you offer in return, if you lose, sorcerer?
If I lose, I commit to remain in your service as a jester for three years!
If I lose, I commit to remain in your service as a jester for three...
WHAT? NO, OUT OF THE QUESTION!
Well, make up your mind!
?!
Let me have a moment to talk with... um... with myself!
Milord, do you really think this is a good idea?
Don't worry, bailiff! That sorcerer's out of his league against my champions! And I'd really like to have him as a jester!
You little, blue dwarf, what are you trying to do? Are you trying to play some Smurf trick on me?
?
?
Come on, Gargamel, what are you thinking? You simply have to convince him! Anyhow, you won't lose, trust me!
That's good because I have no other choice! But know, I'll get revenge!
So?
Well... it's agreed! I mean... Uh... about the challenge!
Aaah... Finally a little activity! Let everything be prepared for this tournament!
© Peyo
35

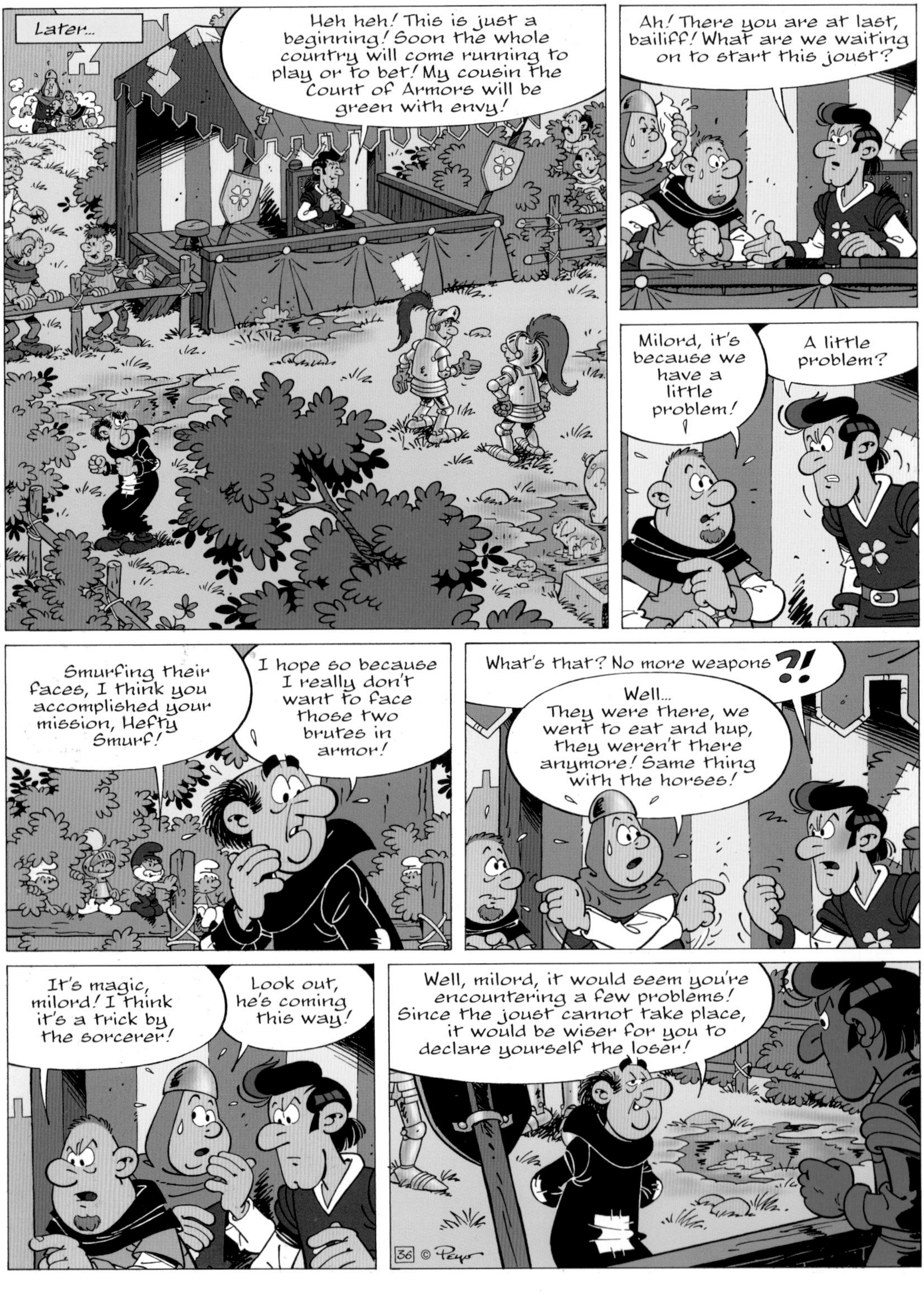
Later...
Heh heh! This is just a beginning! Soon the whole country will come running to play or to bet! My cousin the Count of Armors will be green with envy!
Ah! There you are at last, bailiff! What are we waiting on to start this joust?
Milord, it's because we have a little problem!
A little problem?
Smurfing their faces, I think you accomplished your mission, Hefty Smurf!
I hope so because I really don't want to face those two brutes in armor!
What's that? No more weapons ?!
Well... They were there, we went to eat and hup, they weren't there anymore! Same thing with the horses!
It's magic, milord! I think it's a trick by the sorcerer!
Look out, he's coming this way!
Well, milord, it would seem you're encountering a few problems! Since the joust cannot take place, it would be wiser for you to declare yourself the loser!
36 © Peyo

Run him off, milord! Or have him thrown in the dungeon!

Out of the question! We made a bet and a gambler's word is sacred!

This joust must take place, at all costs...

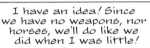

I have an idea! Since we have no weapons, nor horses, we'll do like we did when I was little!

?!

We'll do pigback races, as well as sack races and sack battles! That's what we'll do!

Did you hear, Papa Smurf? What will we smurf?

My plan's falling apart! Gargamel will have to smurf without our help!

Preparations are quickly made, and the first test begins...

HA HA! HEE HEE!

HO HO!

I've never felt so ridiculous! I'll get revenge!

All right, one lap around the village will be enough! Ready?

A little bet, Lucky Smurf?

Okay, but I choose first! I'm tired of losing! I bet Gargamel gets himself smurfed!

Hmm... okay!

It's a deal!

GO!

YEEAAH!

GO!

Go on, run, you filthy hog! If we lose, I'll change you into a sausage!

37

© Peyo

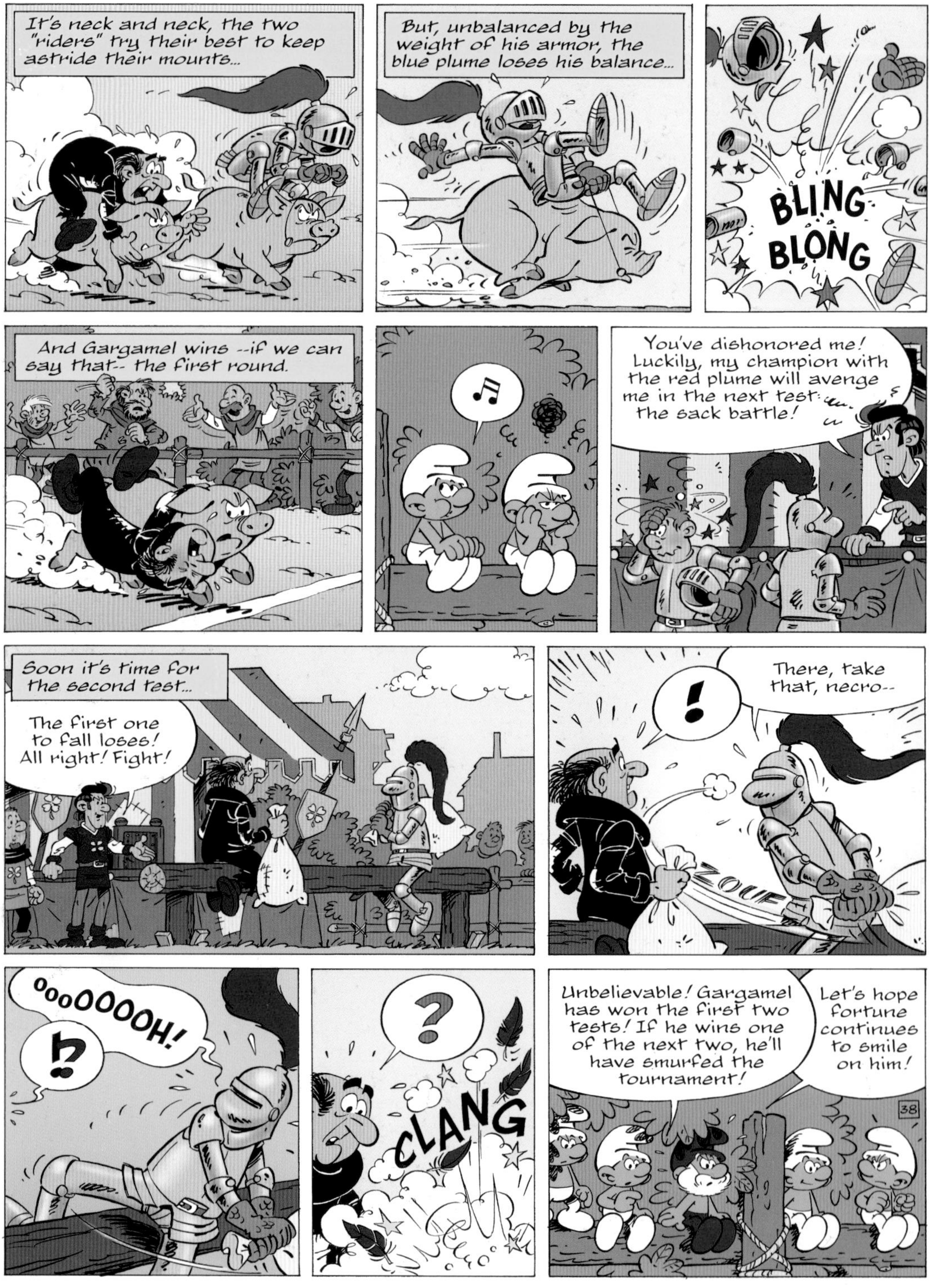

It's neck and neck, the two "riders" try their best to keep astride their mounts...
But, unbalanced by the weight of his armor, the blue plume loses his balance...
BLING
BLONG
And Gargamel wins --if we can say that-- the first round.
♫
You've dishonored me! Luckily, my champion with the red plume will avenge me in the next test: the sack battle!
Soon it's time for the second test...
The first one to fall loses! All right! Fight!
!
There, take that, necro--
ZOUF
oooOOOOH!
!?
?
CLANG
Unbelievable! Gargamel has won the first two tests! If he wins one of the next two, he'll have smurfed the tournament!
Let's hope fortune continues to smile on him!
38

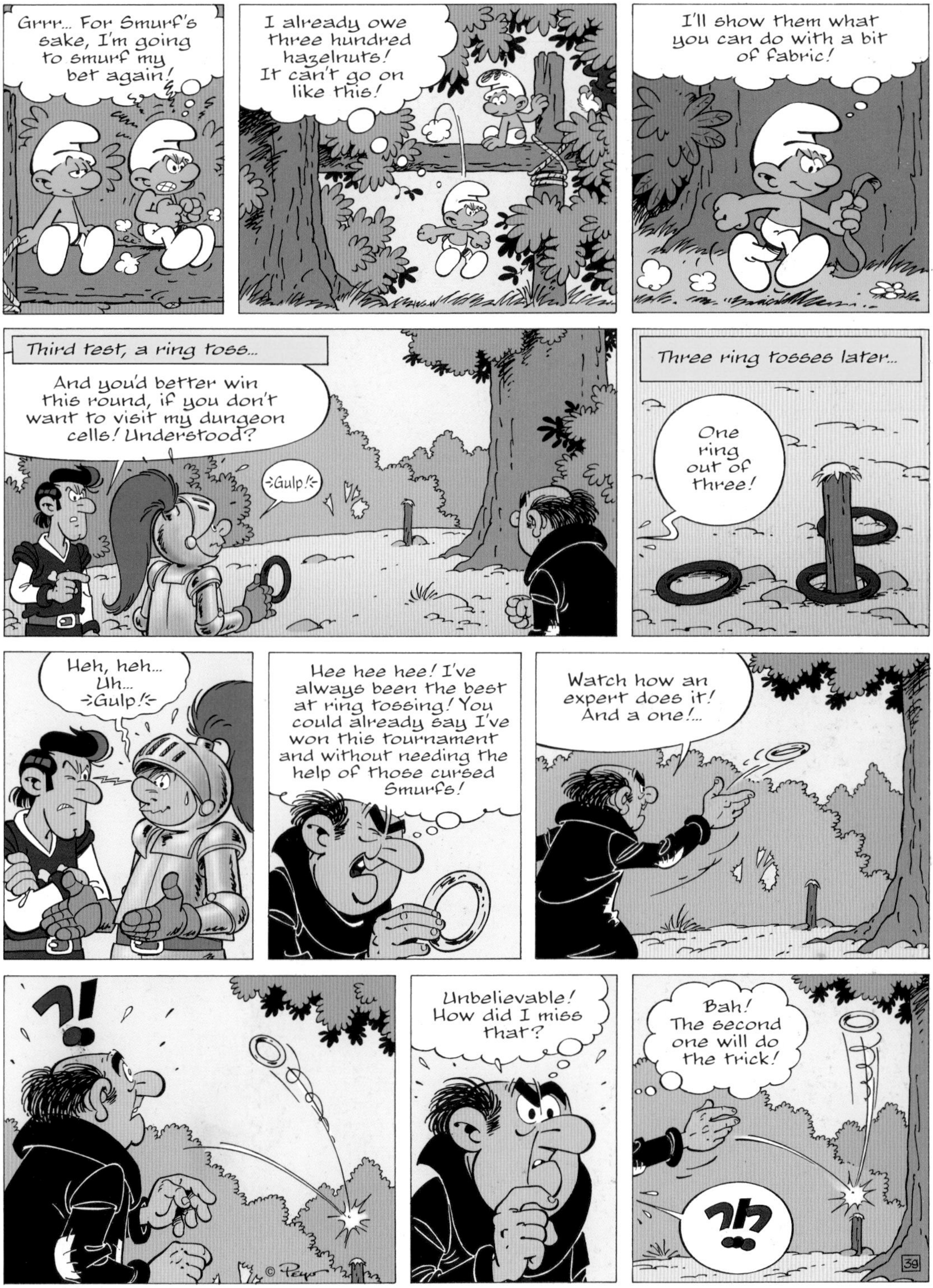

Grrr... For Smurf's sake, I'm going to smurf my bet again!
I already owe three hundred hazelnuts! It can't go on like this!
I'll show them what you can do with a bit of fabric!
Third test, a ring toss...
And you'd better win this round, if you don't want to visit my dungeon cells! Understood?
Gulp!
Three ring tosses later...
One ring out of three!
Heh, heh... Uh... Gulp!
Hee hee hee! I've always been the best at ring tossing! You could already say I've won this tournament and without needing the help of those cursed Smurfs!
Watch how an expert does it! And a one!...
?!
© Peyo
Unbelievable! How did I miss that?
Bah! The second one will do the trick!
?!?
39

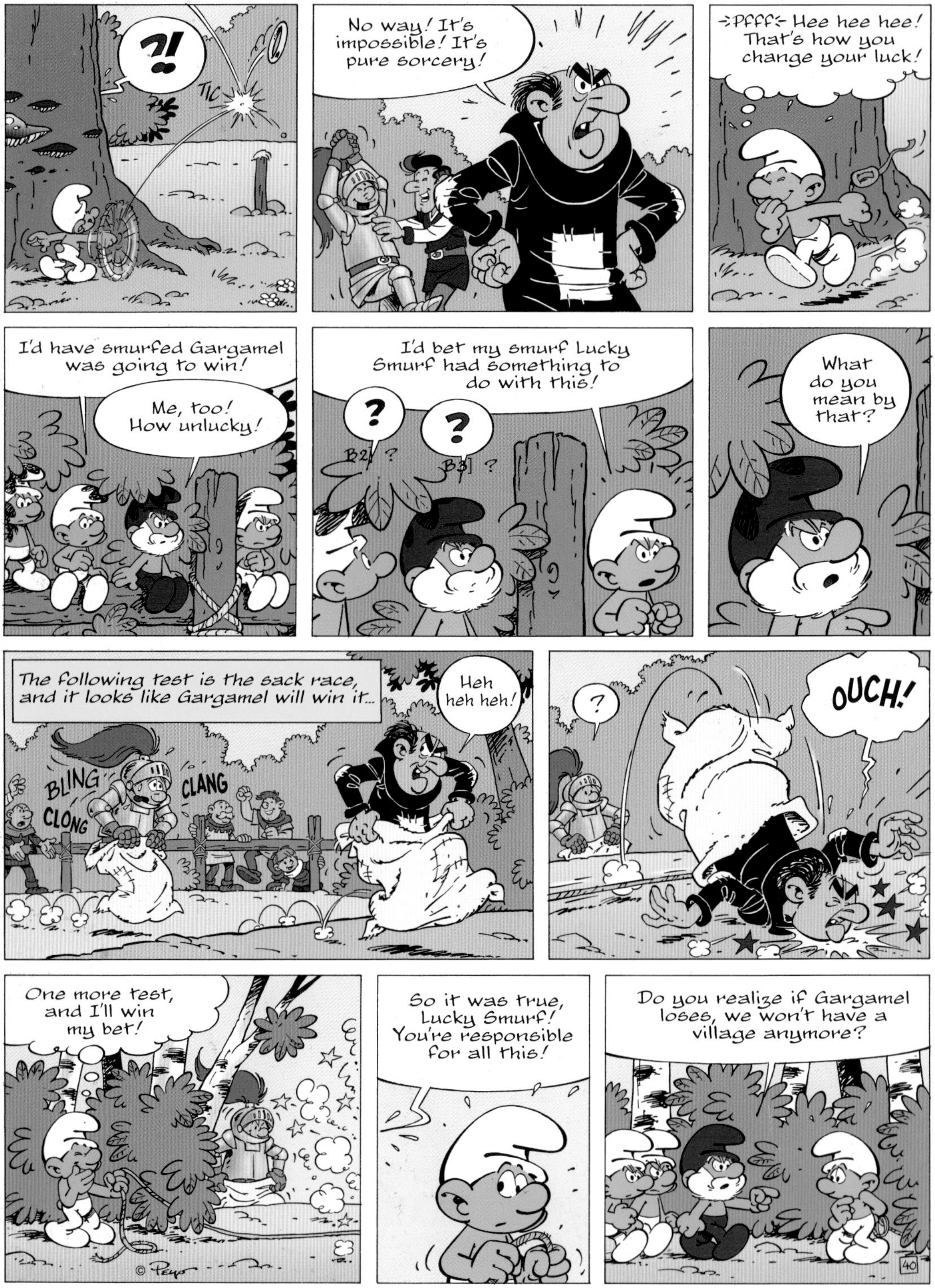
?!
TIC
No way! It's impossible! It's pure sorcery!
Pfff! Hee hee hee! That's how you change your luck!
I'd have smurfed Gargamel was going to win!
Me, too! How unlucky!
I'd bet my smurf Lucky Smurf had something to do with this!
?
?
What do you mean by that?
The following test is the sack race, and it looks like Gargamel will win it...
Heh heh heh!
BLING
CLONG
CLANG
?
OUCH!
One more test, and I'll win my bet!
So it was true, Lucky Smurf! You're responsible for all this!
Do you realize if Gargamel loses, we won't have a village anymore?
© Peyo
40

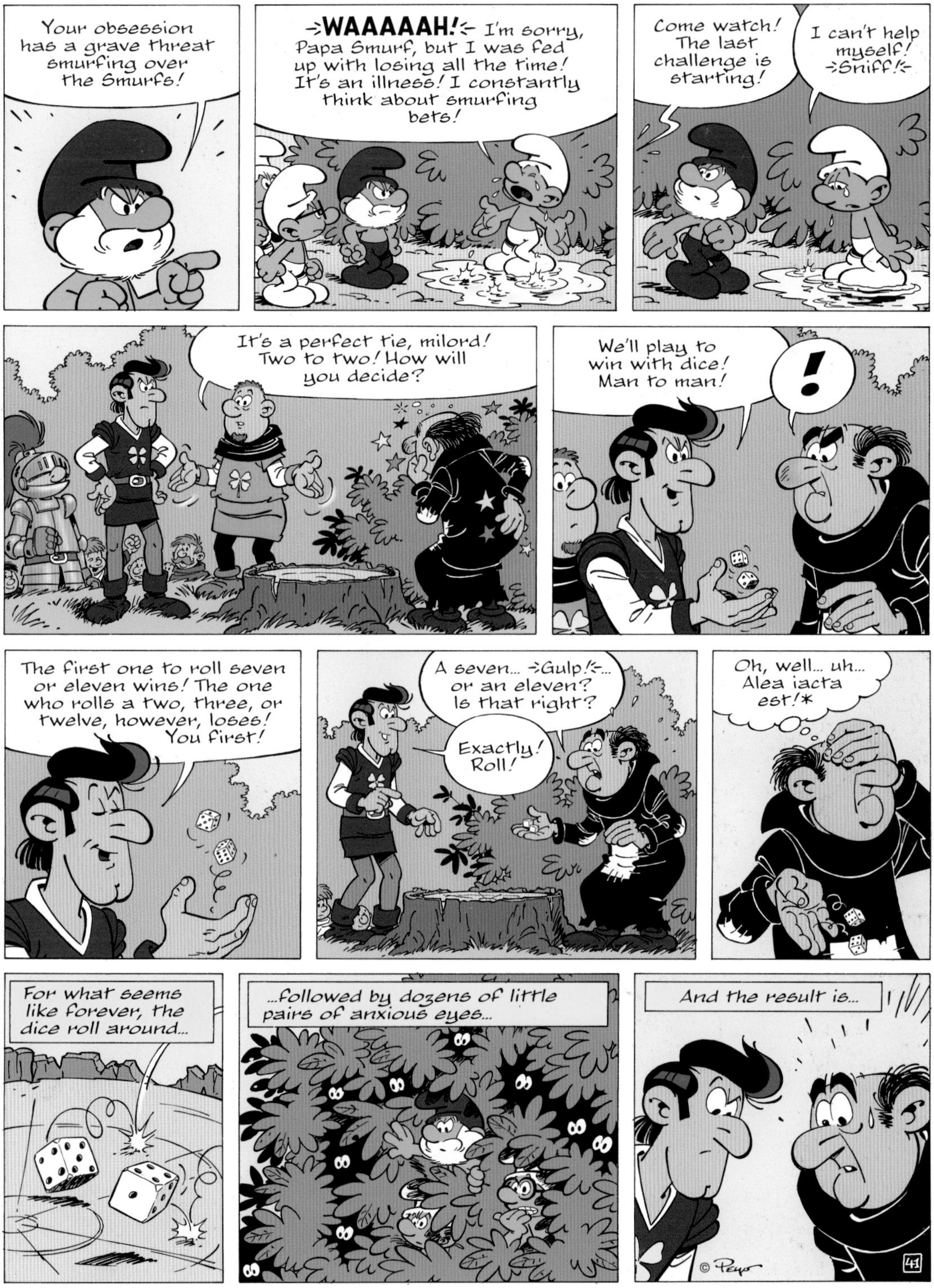

Your obsession has a grave threat smurfing over the Smurfs!
WAAAAAH! I'm sorry, Papa Smurf, but I was fed up with losing all the time! It's an illness! I constantly think about smurfing bets!
Come watch! The last challenge is starting!
I can't help myself! Sniff!
It's a perfect tie, milord! Two to two! How will you decide?
We'll play to win with dice! Man to man!
!
The first one to roll seven or eleven wins! The one who rolls a two, three, or twelve, however, loses! You first!
A seven... Gulp!... or an eleven? Is that right?
Exactly! Roll!
Oh, well... uh... Alea iacta est!*
For what seems like forever, the dice roll around...
...followed by dozens of little pairs of anxious eyes...
And the result is...
© Peyo
41

*Latin: "The die is cast," of course!

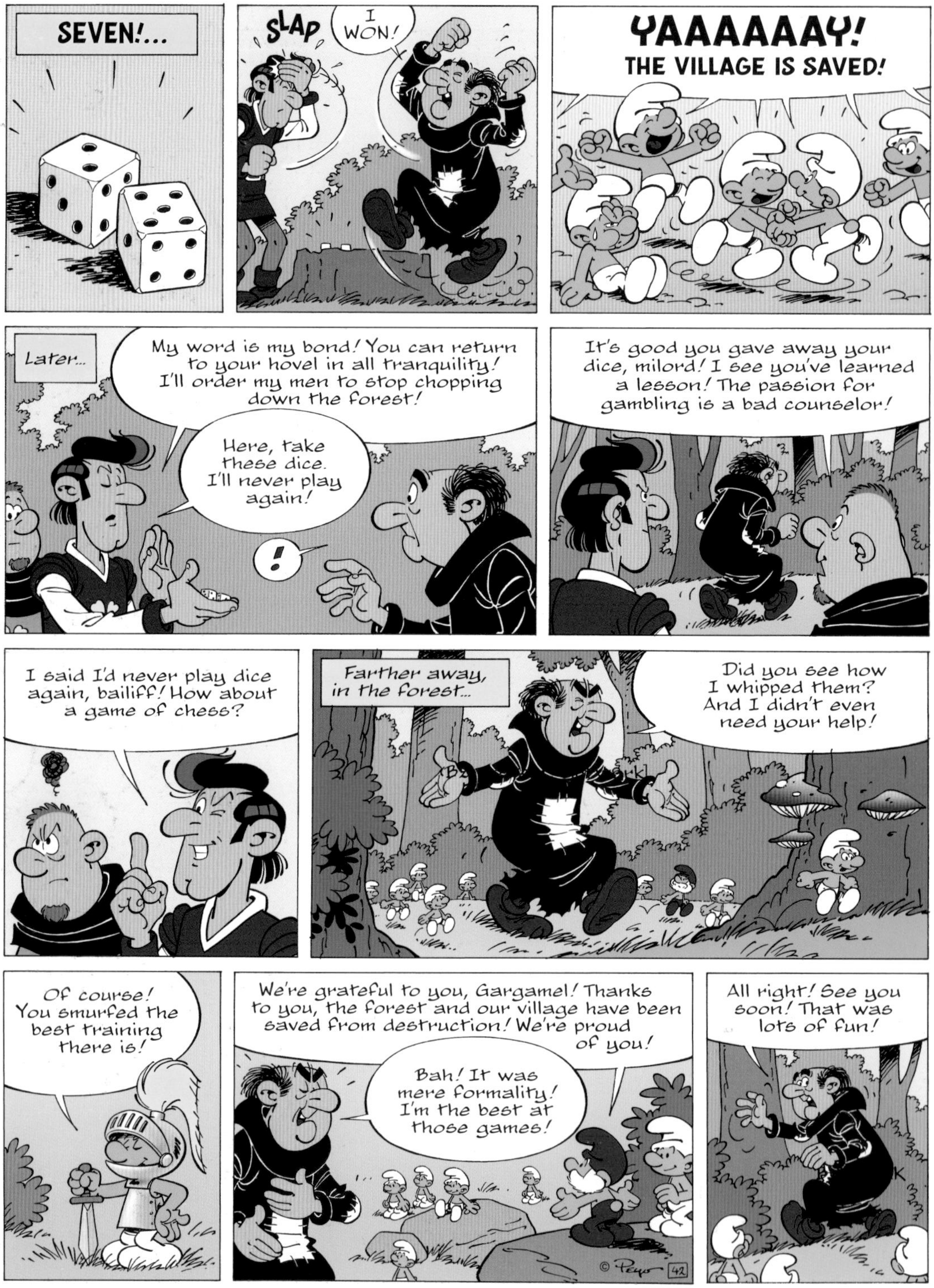
SEVEN!...
SLAP
I WON!
YAAAAAAY!
THE VILLAGE IS SAVED!
Later...
My word is my bond! You can return to your hovel in all tranquility! I'll order my men to stop chopping down the forest!
Here, take these dice. I'll never play again!
!
It's good you gave away your dice, milord! I see you've learned a lesson! The passion for gambling is a bad counselor!
I said I'd never play dice again, bailiff! How about a game of chess?
Farther away, in the forest...
Did you see how I whipped them? And I didn't even need your help!
Of course! You smurfed the best training there is!
We're grateful to you, Gargamel! Thanks to you, the forest and our village have been saved from destruction! We're proud of you!
Bah! It was mere formality! I'm the best at those games!
© Peyo
42
All right! See you soon! That was lots of fun!

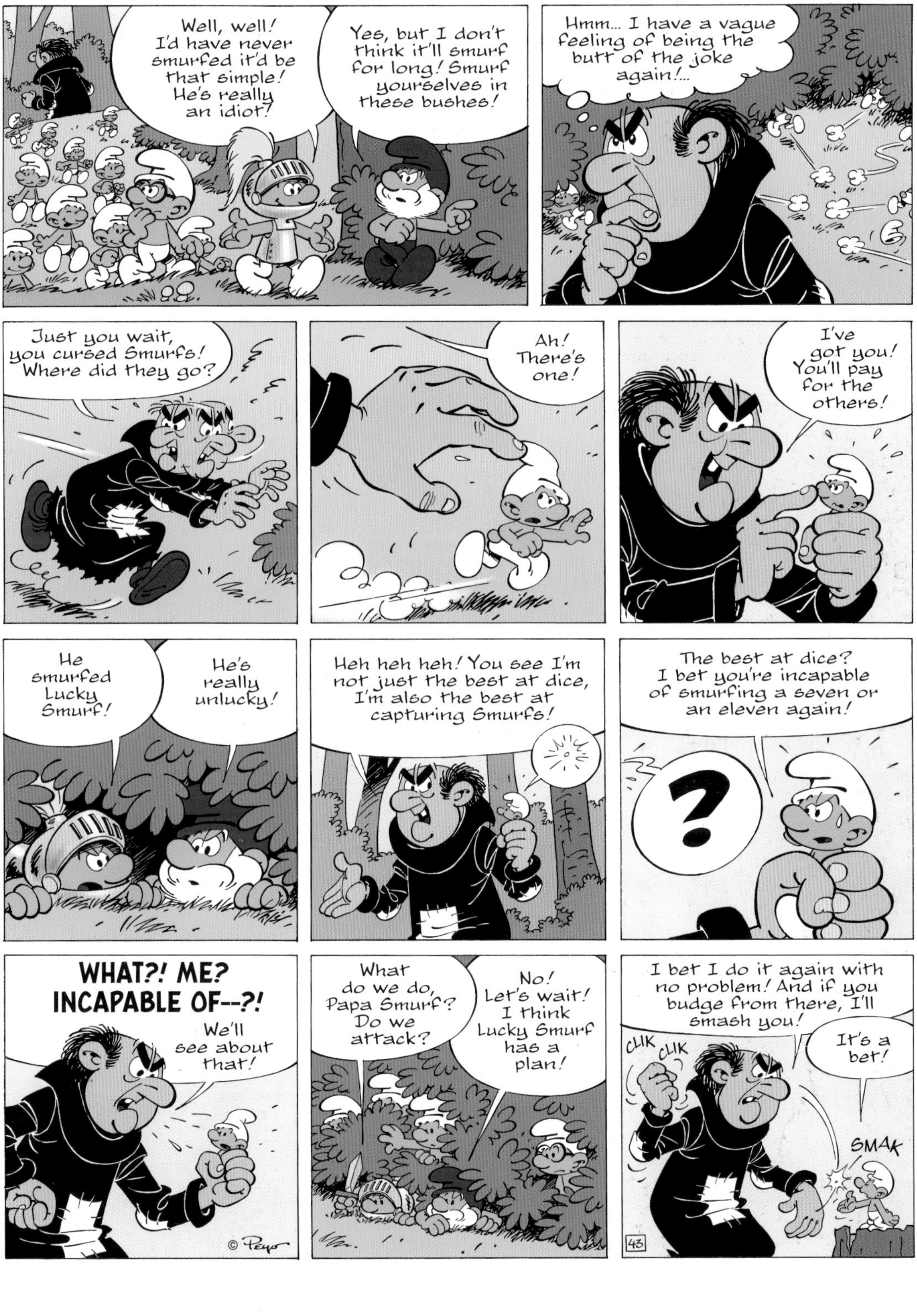

Well, well! I'd have never smurfed it'd be that simple! He's really an idiot!
Yes, but I don't think it'll smurf for long! Smurf yourselves in these bushes!
Hmm... I have a vague feeling of being the butt of the joke again!...
Just you wait, you cursed Smurfs! Where did they go?
Ah! There's one!
I've got you! You'll pay for the others!
He smurfed Lucky Smurf!
He's really unlucky!
Heh heh heh! You see I'm not just the best at dice, I'm also the best at capturing Smurfs!
The best at dice? I bet you're incapable of smurfing a seven or an eleven again!
?
WHAT?! ME? INCAPABLE OF--?!
We'll see about that!
© Peyo
What do we do, Papa Smurf? Do we attack?
No! Let's wait! I think Lucky Smurf has a plan!
I bet I do it again with no problem! And if you budge from there, I'll smash you!
It's a bet!
CLIK
CLIK
SMAK
43

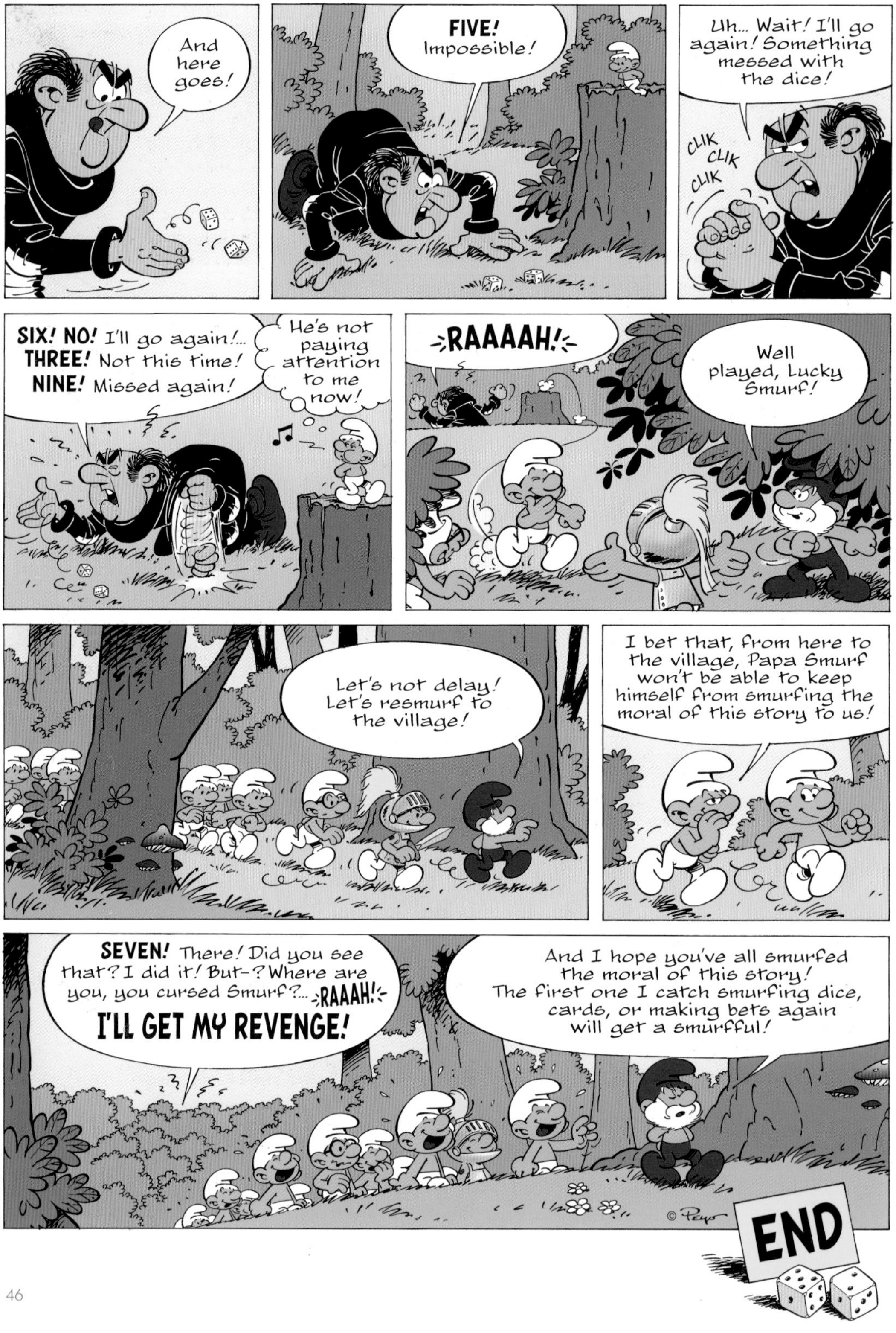
And here goes!
FIVE! Impossible!
Uh... Wait! I'll go again! Something messed with the dice!
CLIK CLIK CLIK
SIX! NO! I'll go again!... THREE! Not this time! NINE! Missed again!
He's not paying attention to me now!
RAAAAH!
Well played, Lucky Smurf!
Let's not delay! Let's resmurf to the village!
I bet that, from here to the village, Papa Smurf won't be able to keep himself from smurfing the moral of this story to us!
SEVEN! There! Did you see that? I did it! But-? Where are you, you cursed Smurf?... RAAAH! I'LL GET MY REVENGE!
And I hope you've all smurfed the moral of this story! The first one I catch smurfing dice, cards, or making bets again will get a smurfful!
© Peyo
END

WATCH OUT FOR PAPERCUTZ

If you bet that I was going to start this page by writing, "Welcome to the tournament-wagering twenty-fifth SMURFS graphic novel by Peyo, from Papercutz, those poker-faced people dedicated to publishing great graphic novels for all ages." Then you just won your bet[1]. But can you tell me how you knew? Because if you could've told me what I was going to write, it would've saved me a little time! Oh, and I'm Jim Salicrup, by the way, the lucky scratch card-playing Smurf-in-Chief, with some smurfy reflections on our 25th Smuferversary…

We're all smurfcited that this is our 25th SMURFS graphic novel, not counting all THE SMURFS specials, THE SMURFS AND FRIENDS, THE SMURFS ANTHOLOGY, and all the other SMURFS books (and comicbooks) we've been proudly publishing since 2010. Believe it or not, when we at Papercutz first launched our first two SMURFS graphic novels, we had no idea if the series would sell well enough to allow us to publish any further volumes. We certainly hoped it would, but being a relatively small publisher (about three apples tall) constantly battling for survival against our much bigger competitors, we can never be certain. Let's face it, publishing is like gambling. With every graphic novel Papercutz publishes, we can either win or lose. When we lose, we hope we're able to move on and try publishing other graphic novels that will fare better. If we win, we get to publish more of the graphic novels we love.

Fortunately, our betting on THE SMURFS paid off big-time, but I still remember thinking that those two initial SMURFS graphic novels might've been the only SMURFS graphic novels ever published by Papercutz. Therefore I had to carefully choose the two most wanted to see published in North America. It was like a Smurf-genie was granting me only two wishes. The first choice was easy: "The Purple Smurfs." While most of THE SMURFS graphic novels had been translated into English at some point, this one never had been[2], despite being adapted into one of the early episodes on the hit, long-running Saturday morning animated TV series. The second choice was tough too: "The Smurfs and the Magic Flute." This wasn't even technically a SMURFS story, it was an episode of Peyo's *Johan and Peewit* series, but it was the story that first introduced the Smurfs over sixty years ago, How could we not want to publish this one?

Which brings us back to this 25th Papercutz SMURFS graphic novel, and in addition to featuring "The Gambling Smurfs," we're presenting the conclusion to "The Flute Smurfers," the special prequel to "The Smurfs and the Magic Flute." This story was originally created ten years ago, just a year or so before Papercutz started publishing THE SMURFS, to celebrate the fiftieth anniversary of THE SMURFS. We presented it in its entirety in THE SMURFS AND FRIENDS Volume One, but we thought it would be fun to re-present it to both celebrate the sixtieth anniversary of THE SMURFS in THE SMURFS #24 and here to celebrate our twenty-fifth volume of THE SMURFS!

Now if it turns out that you missed "The Smurfs and the Magic Flute," and you want to see what happens next after "The Flute Smurfers," don't worry—you have loads of options. You can either go to your favorite bookstore, library, or online (www.comixology.com, for example) and find that story in any one of the following: THE SMURFS #2 "The Smurfs and the Magic Flute," THE SMURFS 3 IN 1 #1, or THE SMURFS ANTHOLOGY Volume One. And if you've already enjoyed that classic tale, be sure to join us for THE SMURFS #26 "Smurf Salad," and don't forget to look for the all-new Smurfs animated series, both coming soon! There's never any reason to be without Smurfs!

Smurf you later

[1]Of course, we at Papercutz don't encourage gambling of any kind, but if you do ever gamble, our advice is to never bet more than you can afford to lose.
[2]For the full story, check out Smurfologist Matt. Murray's introduction to "The Purple Smurfs" in THE SMURFS ANTHOLOGY Volume One.

STAY IN TOUCH!

EMAIL:	salicrup@papercutz.com
WEB:	papercutz.com
TWITTER:	@papercutzgn
INSTAGRAM:	@papercutzgn
FACEBOOK:	PAPERCUTZGRAPHICNOVELS
FANMAIL:	Papercutz, 160 Broadway, Suite 700, East Wing, New York, NY 10038

THE FLUTE SMURFERS Conclusion

PREVIOUSLY IN THE SMURFS #24…

A stork arrived at the Smurf Village with an important message for Papa Smurf from his friend, the sorcerer Alderic, asking him to create a magic flute. The magic flute would be to cure one of his patients with a "Monotone Melancholy," an illness that humans are especially susceptible to which fills them with apathy to the point that they'll not make the slightest move all day long. The Smurfs create the magic flute and deliver it to him. Alderic explains to Papa Smurf that Emile, a peasant, contracted the illness after carelessly walking through a fairy ring. With the village doctor unable to help Emile, his wife came to Alderic for help. The Smurfs and the sorcerer bring the magic flute to Emile's home, play the flute, and the peasant hops out of bed cured! Little did they know that the village doctor was right outside the house and witnessed Emile's remarkable recovery. The doctor, scheming to get rid of Alderic, decides he must have the magic flute. After Alderic and the Smurfs leave, Papa Smurf realizes he forgot to give Emile an important bit of advice, and rushes back alone to the peasant's home. He's ambushed by the village doctor, who knocks out Papa Smurf and takes the magic flute. The Smurfs decide they must enter the village, to reclaim the flute. They see their chance to hop on a coalman's cart as he's entering the village…

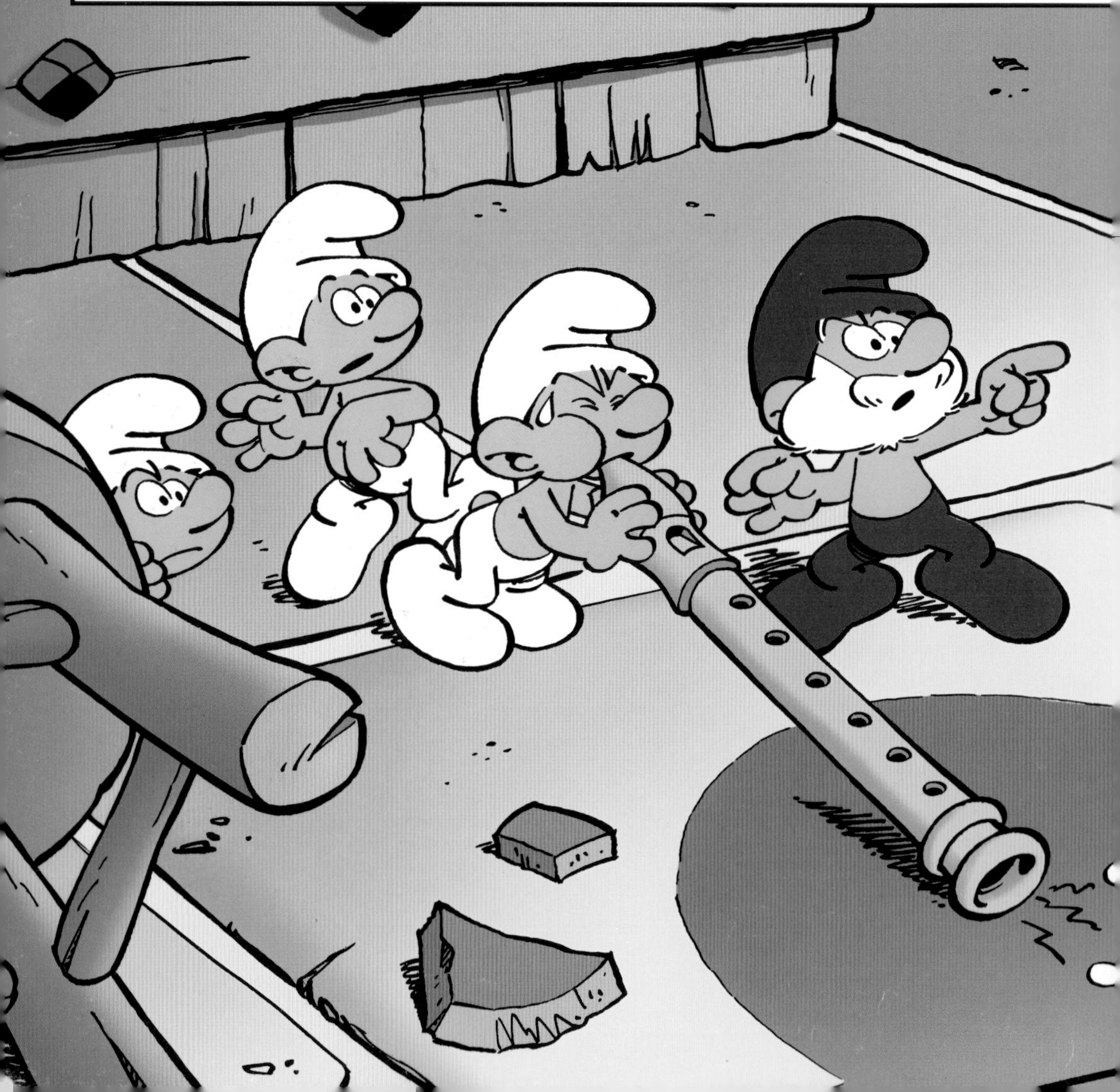

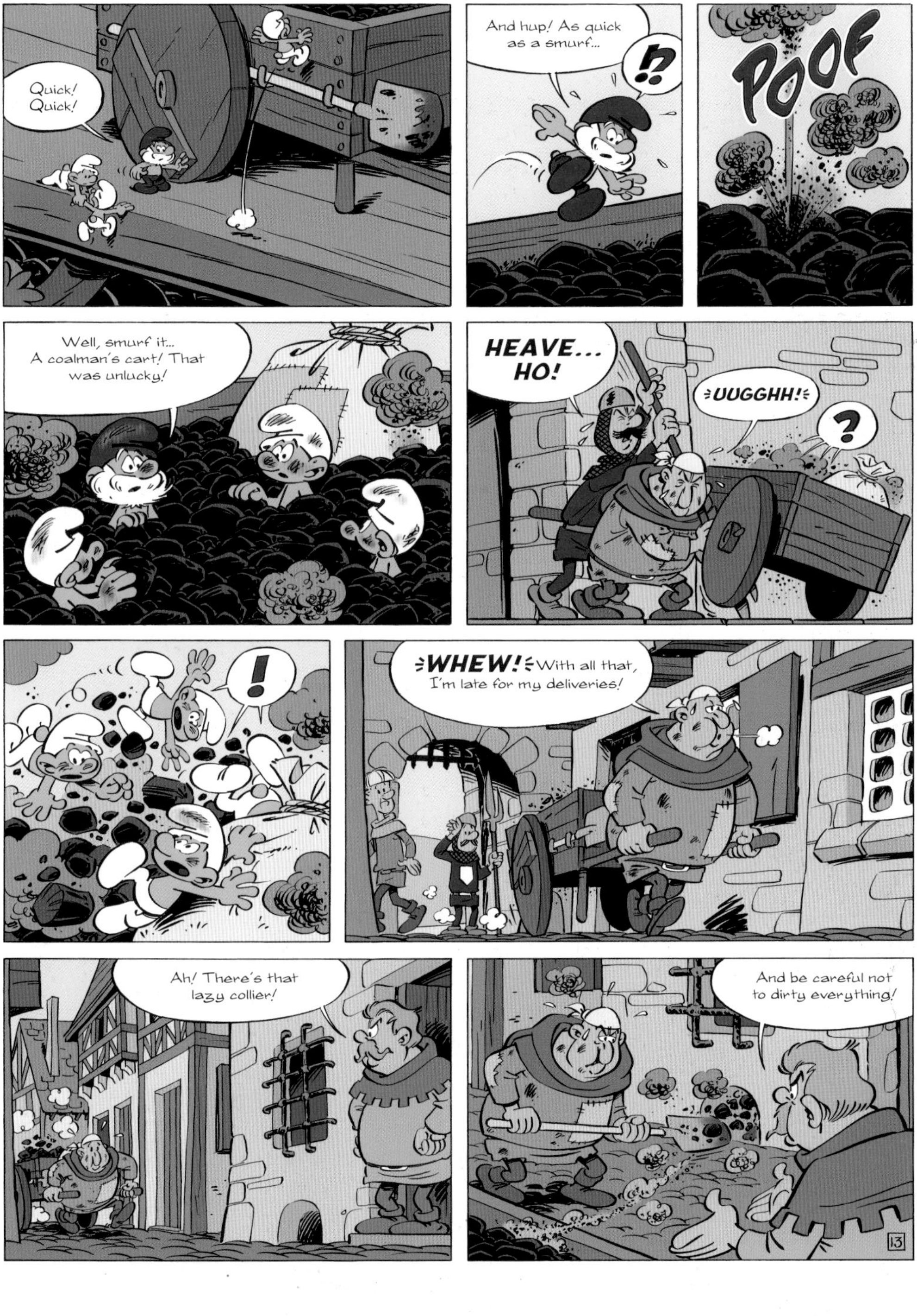
Quick! Quick!
And hup! As quick as a smurf...
!?
POOF
Well, smurf it... A coalman's cart! That was unlucky!
HEAVE... HO!
UUGGHH!
?
!
WHEW! With all that, I'm late for my deliveries!
Ah! There's that lazy collier!
And be careful not to dirty everything!
13

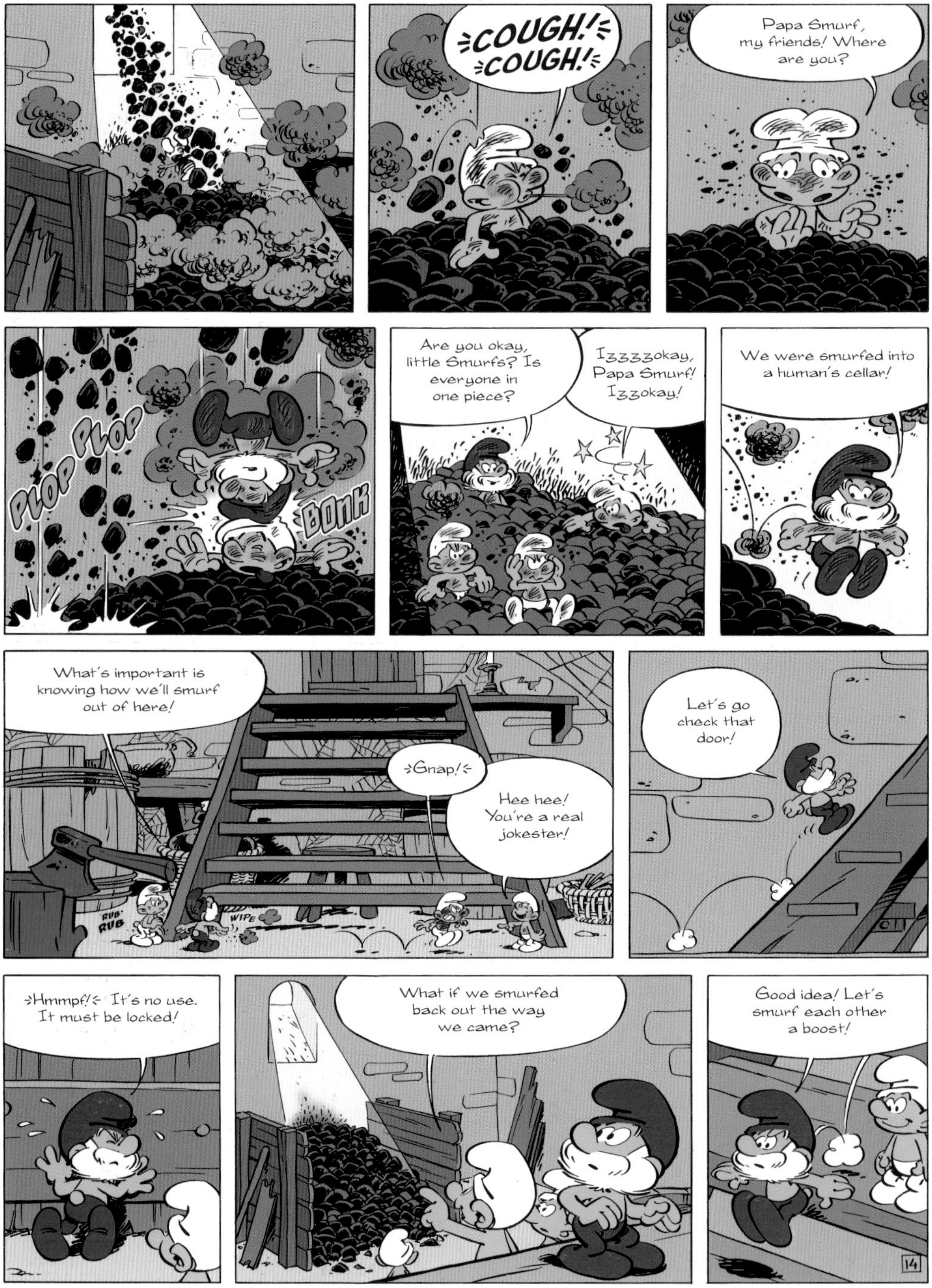
COUGH! COUGH!
Papa Smurf, my friends! Where are you?
PLOP PLOP
BONK
Are you okay, little Smurfs? Is everyone in one piece?
Izzzzokay, Papa Smurf! Izzokay!
We were smurfed into a human's cellar!
What's important is knowing how we'll smurf out of here!
Gnap!
Hee hee! You're a real jokester!
RUB RUB
WIPE
Let's go check that door!
Hmmpf! It's no use. It must be locked!
What if we smurfed back out the way we came?
Good idea! Let's smurf each other a boost!
14

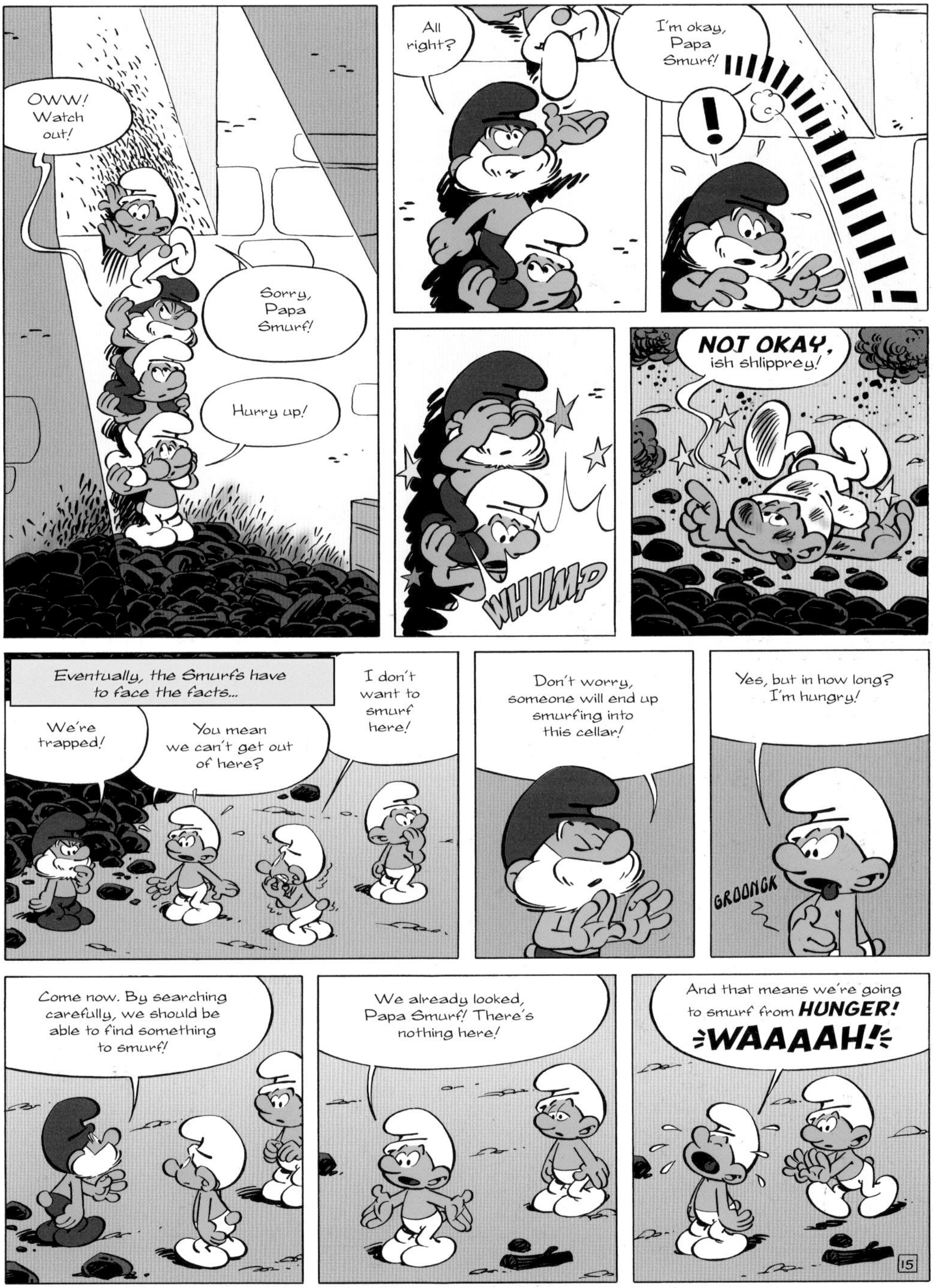
OWW! Watch out!
Sorry, Papa Smurf!
Hurry up!
All right?
I'm okay, Papa Smurf!
!
WHUMP
NOT OKAY, ish shlipprey!
Eventually, the Smurfs have to face the facts...
We're trapped!
You mean we can't get out of here?
I don't want to smurf here!
Don't worry, someone will end up smurfing into this cellar!
Yes, but in how long? I'm hungry!
GROONGK
Come now. By searching carefully, we should be able to find something to smurf!
We already looked, Papa Smurf! There's nothing here!
And that means we're going to smurf from HUNGER!
WAAAAH!
15

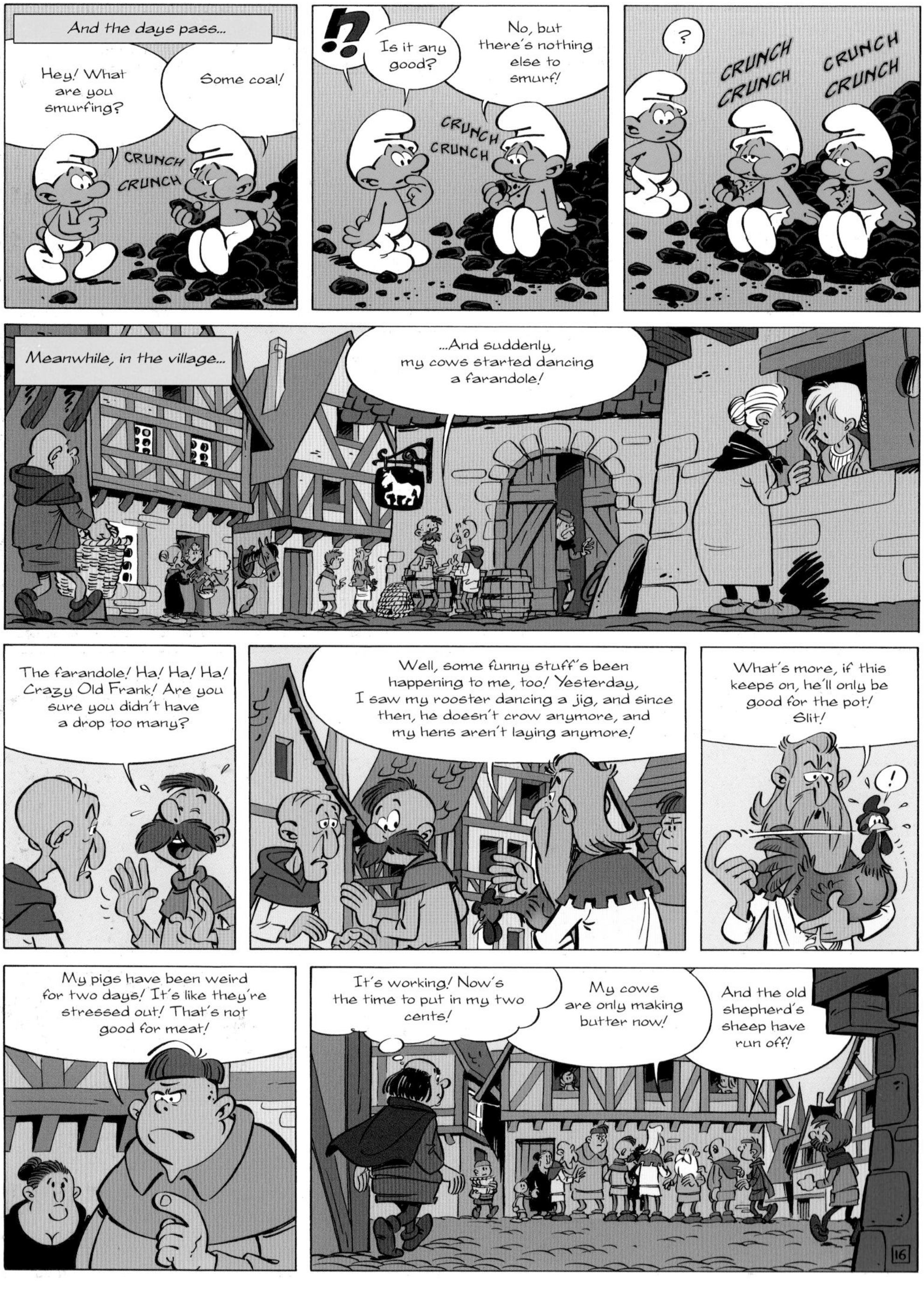
And the days pass...
Hey! What are you smurfing?
Some coal!
CRUNCH CRUNCH
!?
Is it any good?
No, but there's nothing else to smurf!
CRUNCH CRUNCH
?
CRUNCH CRUNCH
CRUNCH CRUNCH
Meanwhile, in the village...
...And suddenly, my cows started dancing a farandole!
The farandole! Ha! Ha! Ha! Crazy Old Frank! Are you sure you didn't have a drop too many?
Well, some funny stuff's been happening to me, too! Yesterday, I saw my rooster dancing a jig, and since then, he doesn't crow anymore, and my hens aren't laying anymore!
What's more, if this keeps on, he'll only be good for the pot! Slit!
!
My pigs have been weird for two days! It's like they're stressed out! That's not good for meat!
It's working! Now's the time to put in my two cents!
My cows are only making butter now!
And the old shepherd's sheep have run off!
16

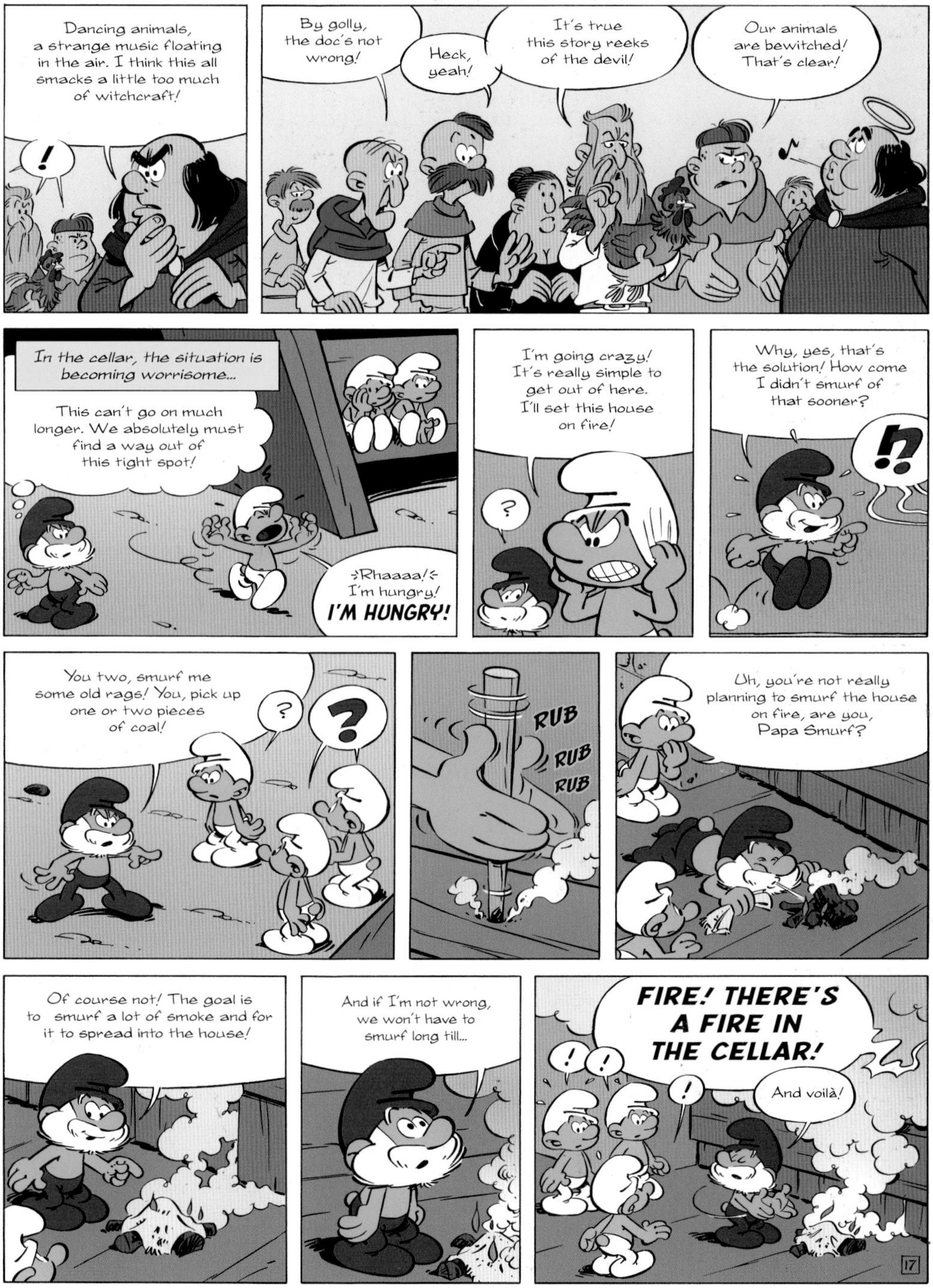

Dancing animals, a strange music floating in the air. I think this all smacks a little too much of witchcraft!
!
By golly, the doc's not wrong!
Heck, yeah!
It's true this story reeks of the devil!
Our animals are bewitched! That's clear!
In the cellar, the situation is becoming worrisome...
This can't go on much longer. We absolutely must find a way out of this tight spot!
Rhaaaa! I'm hungry! I'M HUNGRY!
I'm going crazy! It's really simple to get out of here. I'll set this house on fire!
?
Why, yes, that's the solution! How come I didn't smurf of that sooner?
!?
You two, smurf me some old rags! You, pick up one or two pieces of coal!
?
?
RUB
RUB
RUB
Uh, you're not really planning to smurf the house on fire, are you, Papa Smurf?
Of course not! The goal is to smurf a lot of smoke and for it to spread into the house!
And if I'm not wrong, we won't have to smurf long till...
FIRE! THERE'S A FIRE IN THE CELLAR!
!
!
!
And voilà!
17

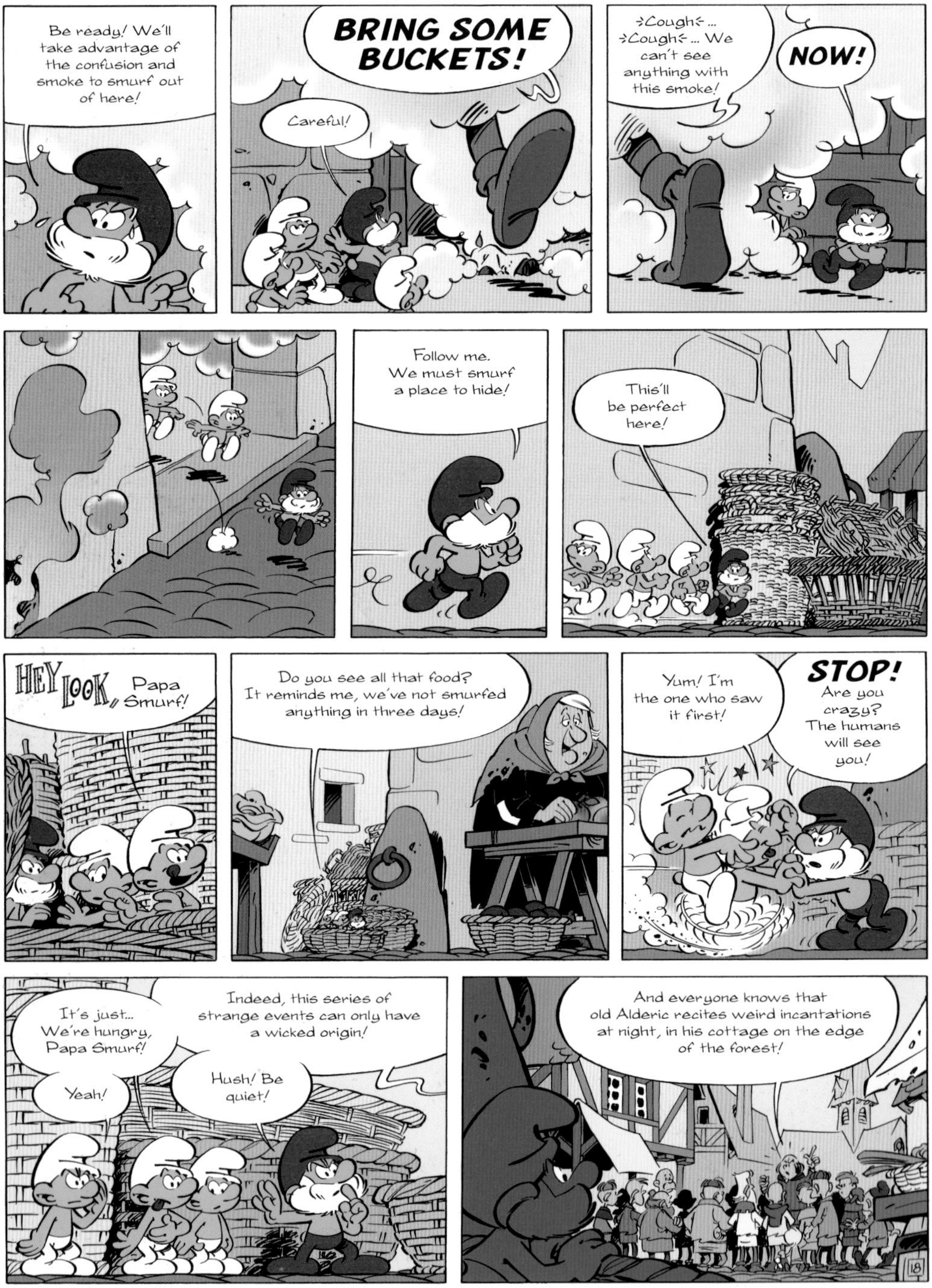

Be ready! We'll take advantage of the confusion and smoke to smurf out of here!
BRING SOME BUCKETS!
Careful!
Cough ... *Cough* ... We can't see anything with this smoke!
NOW!
Follow me. We must smurf a place to hide!
This'll be perfect here!
HEY LOOK, Papa Smurf!
Do you see all that food? It reminds me, we've not smurfed anything in three days!
Yum! I'm the one who saw it first!
STOP! Are you crazy? The humans will see you!
It's just... We're hungry, Papa Smurf!
Yeah!
Indeed, this series of strange events can only have a wicked origin!
Hush! Be quiet!
And everyone knows that old Alderic recites weird incantations at night, in his cottage on the edge of the forest!
18

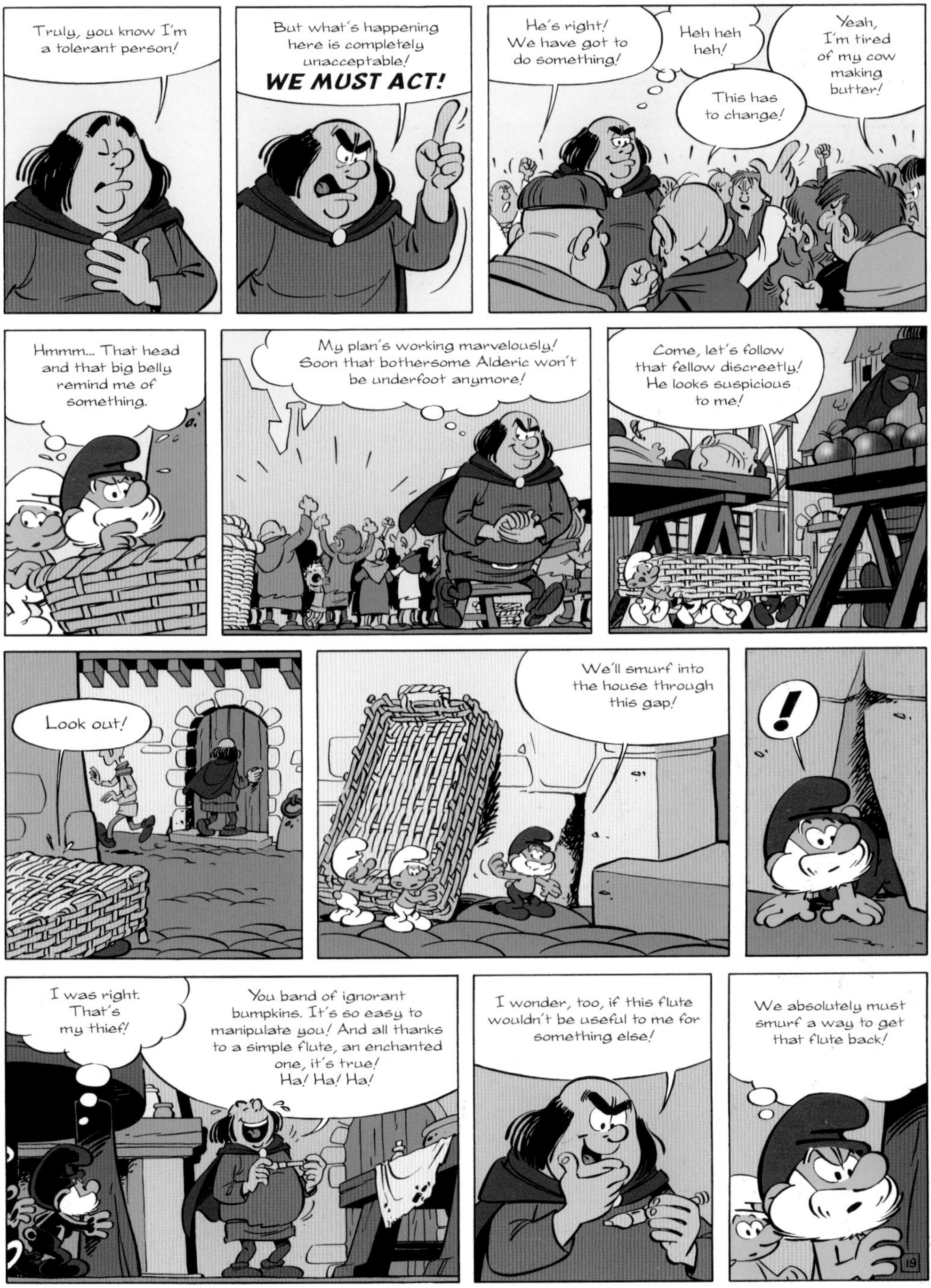
Truly, you know I'm a tolerant person!
But what's happening here is completely unacceptable! WE MUST ACT!
He's right! We have got to do something!
Heh heh heh!
This has to change!
Yeah, I'm tired of my cow making butter!
Hmmm... That head and that big belly remind me of something.
My plan's working marvelously! Soon that bothersome Alderic won't be underfoot anymore!
Come, let's follow that fellow discreetly! He looks suspicious to me!
Look out!
We'll smurf into the house through this gap!
!
I was right. That's my thief!
You band of ignorant bumpkins. It's so easy to manipulate you! And all thanks to a simple flute, an enchanted one, it's true! Ha! Ha! Ha!
I wonder, too, if this flute wouldn't be useful to me for something else!
We absolutely must smurf a way to get that flute back!
19

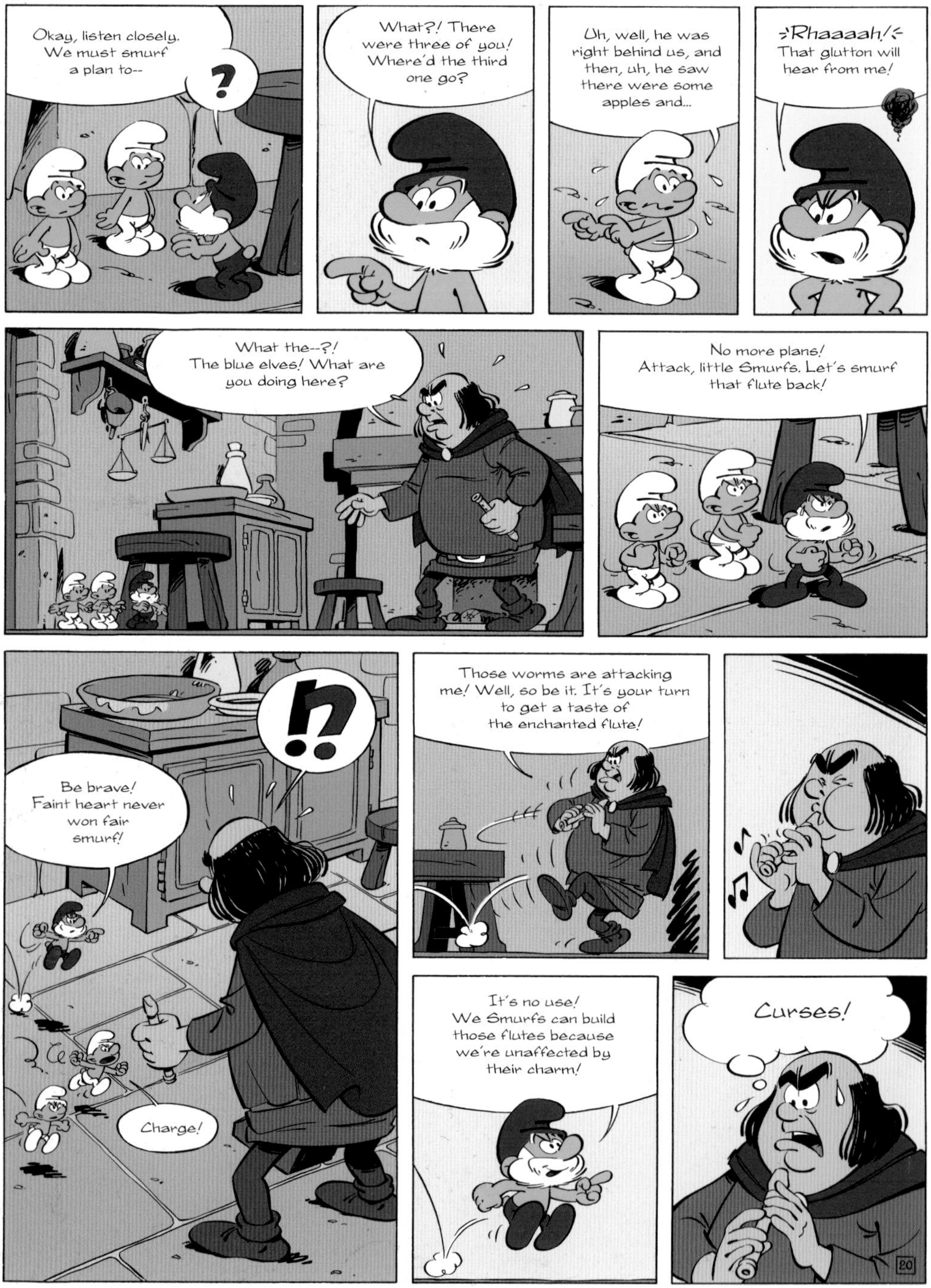
Okay, listen closely. We must smurf a plan to--
?
What?! There were three of you! Where'd the third one go?
Uh, well, he was right behind us, and then, uh, he saw there were some apples and...
Rhaaaah! That glutton will hear from me!
What the--?! The blue elves! What are you doing here?
No more plans! Attack, little Smurfs. Let's smurf that flute back!
!?
Be brave! Faint heart never won fair smurf!
Charge!
Those worms are attacking me! Well, so be it. It's your turn to get a taste of the enchanted flute!
It's no use! We Smurfs can build those flutes because we're unaffected by their charm!
Curses!
20

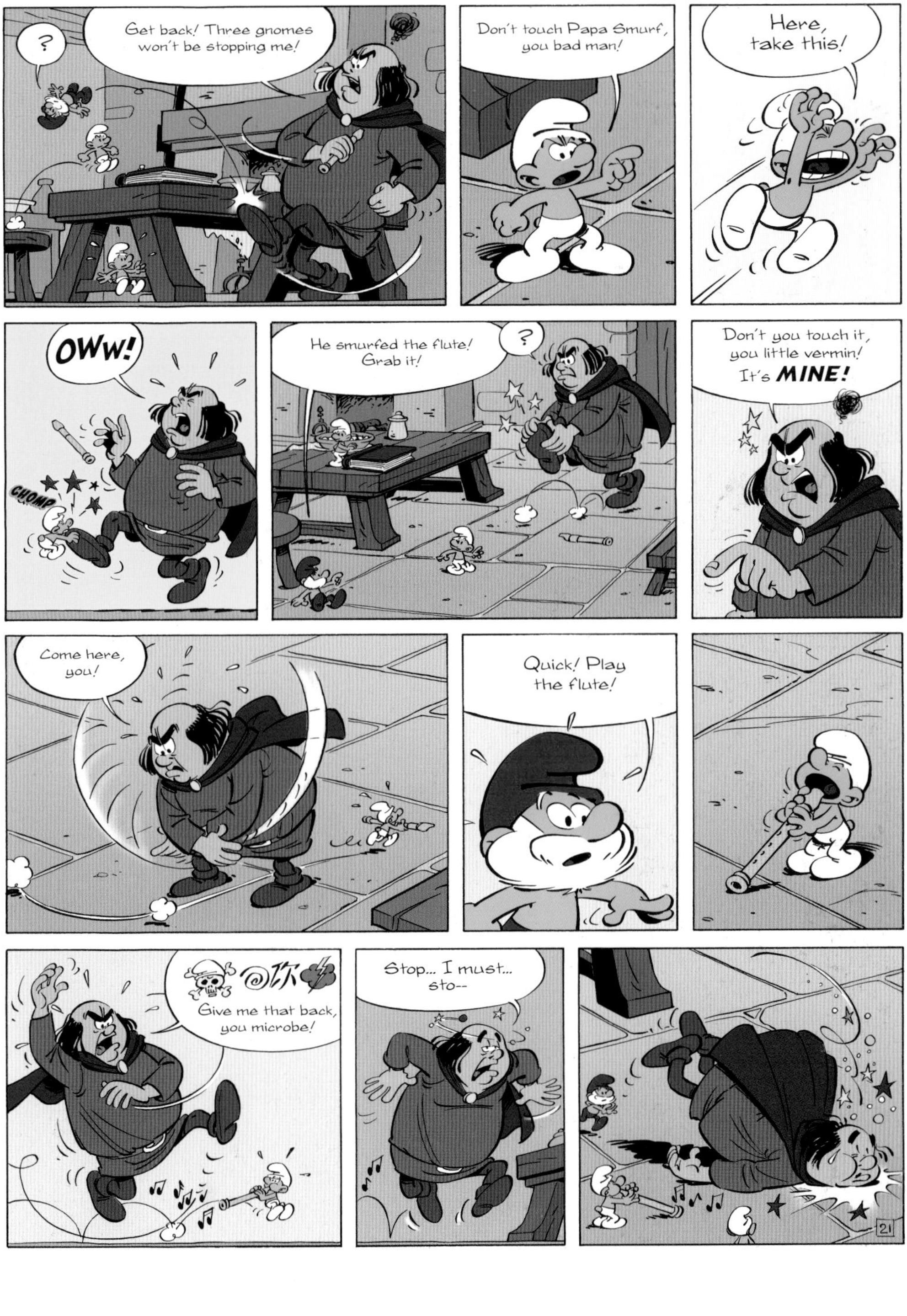
?
Get back! Three gnomes won't be stopping me!
Don't touch Papa Smurf, you bad man!
Here, take this!
OWW!
CHOMP
He smurfed the flute! Grab it!
?
Don't you touch it, you little vermin! It's **MINE!**
Come here, you!
Quick! Play the flute!
Give me that back, you microbe!
Stop... I must... sto--
21

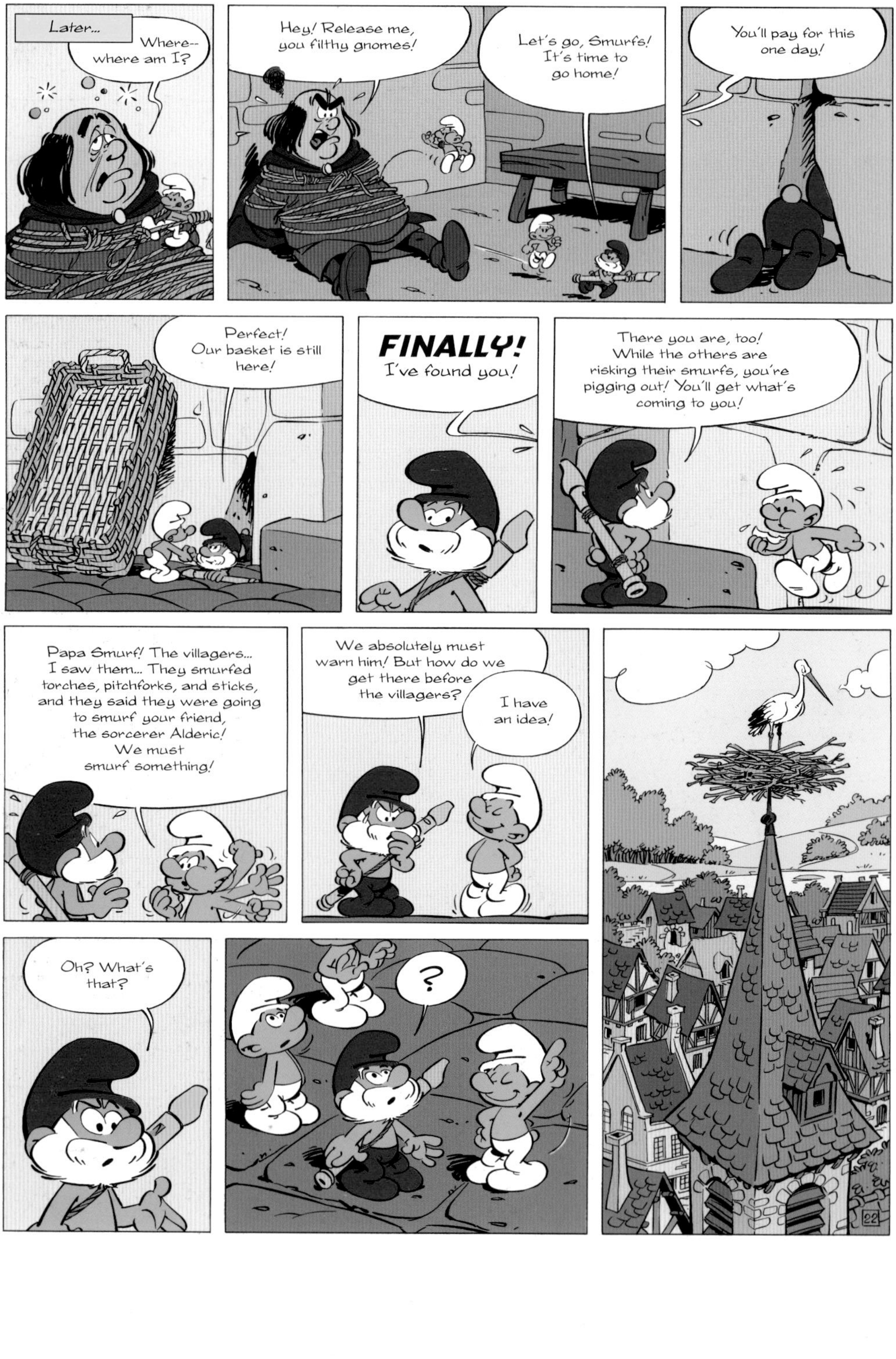
Later...
Where-- where am I?
Hey! Release me, you filthy gnomes!
Let's go, Smurfs! It's time to go home!
You'll pay for this one day!
Perfect! Our basket is still here!
FINALLY! I've found you!
There you are, too! While the others are risking their smurfs, you're pigging out! You'll get what's coming to you!
Papa Smurf! The villagers... I saw them... They smurfed torches, pitchforks, and sticks, and they said they were going to smurf your friend, the sorcerer Alderic! We must smurf something!
We absolutely must warn him! But how do we get there before the villagers?
I have an idea!
22
Oh? What's that?
?

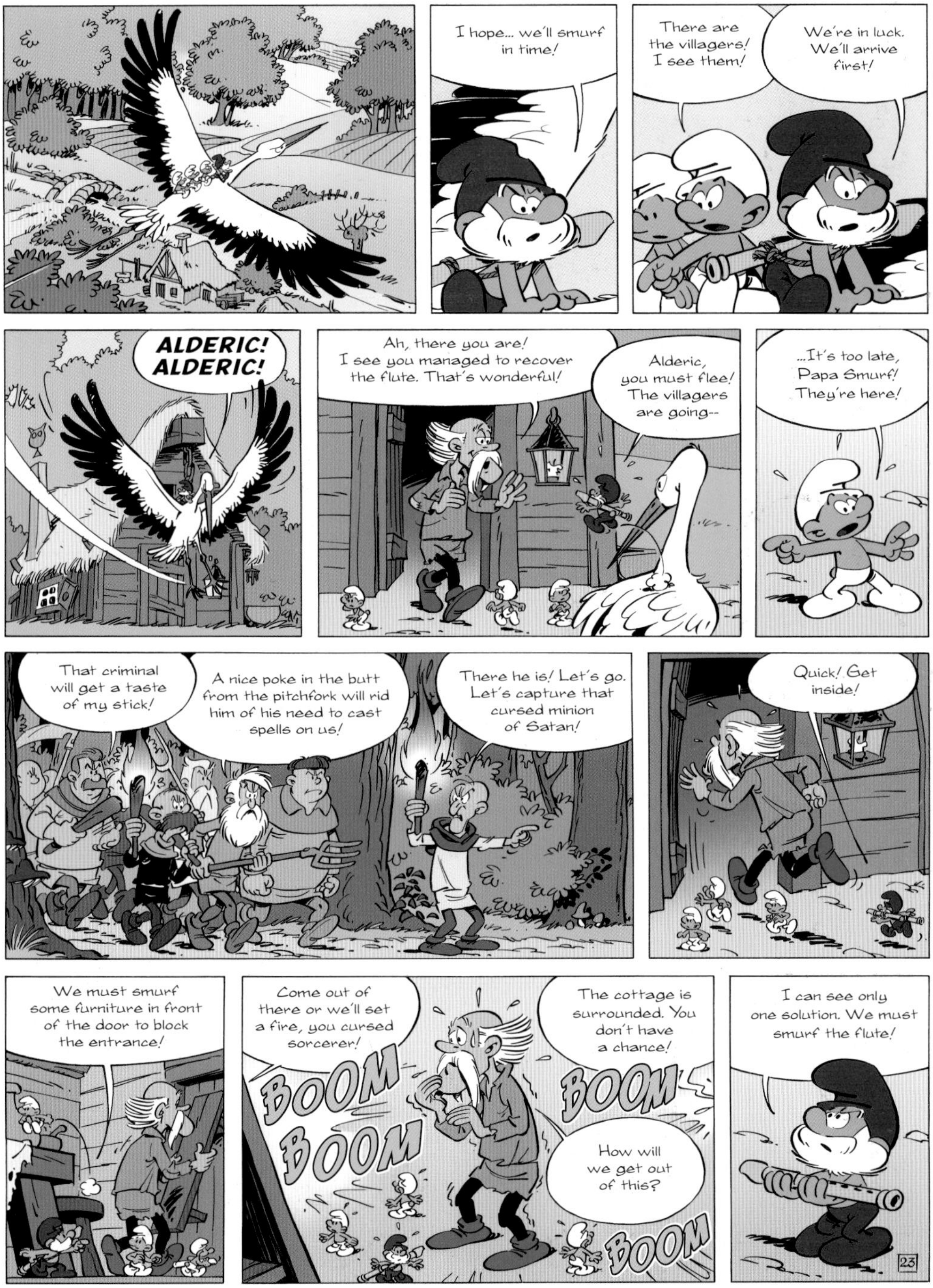
I hope... we'll smurf in time!
There are the villagers! I see them!
We're in luck. We'll arrive first!
ALDERIC! ALDERIC!
Ah, there you are! I see you managed to recover the flute. That's wonderful!
Alderic, you must flee! The villagers are going--
...It's too late, Papa Smurf! They're here!
That criminal will get a taste of my stick!
A nice poke in the butt from the pitchfork will rid him of his need to cast spells on us!
There he is! Let's go. Let's capture that cursed minion of Satan!
Quick! Get inside!
We must smurf some furniture in front of the door to block the entrance!
Come out of there or we'll set a fire, you cursed sorcerer!
BOOM
BOOM
The cottage is surrounded. You don't have a chance!
BOOM
How will we get out of this?
BOOM
I can see only one solution. We must smurf the flute!
23

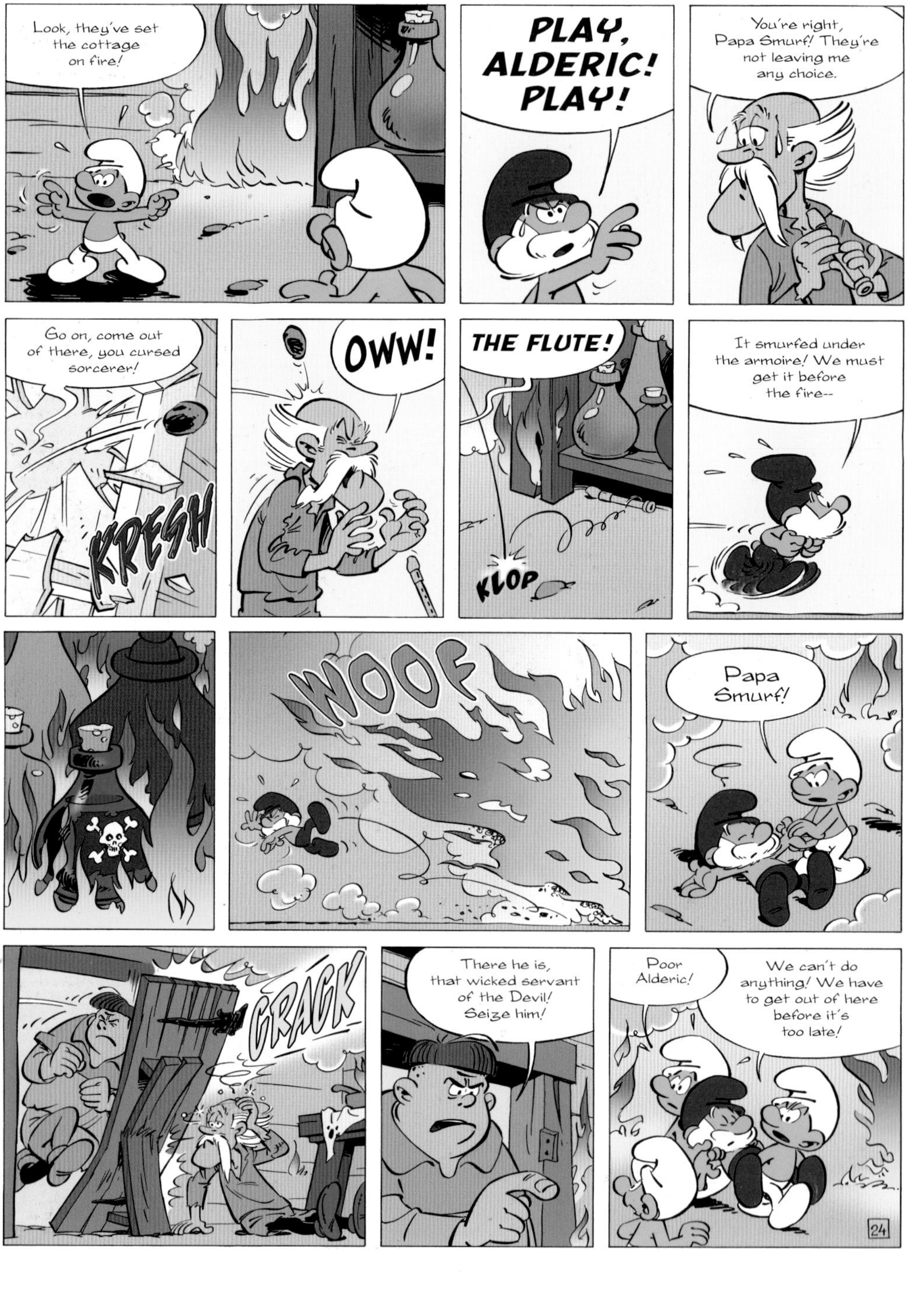

Look, they've set the cottage on fire!
PLAY, ALDERIC! PLAY!
You're right, Papa Smurf! They're not leaving me any choice.
Go on, come out of there, you cursed sorcerer!
KRESH
OWW!
THE FLUTE!
KLOP
It smurfed under the armoire! We must get it before the fire--
WOOF
Papa Smurf!
CRACK
There he is, that wicked servant of the Devil! Seize him!
Poor Alderic!
We can't do anything! We have to get out of here before it's too late!
24

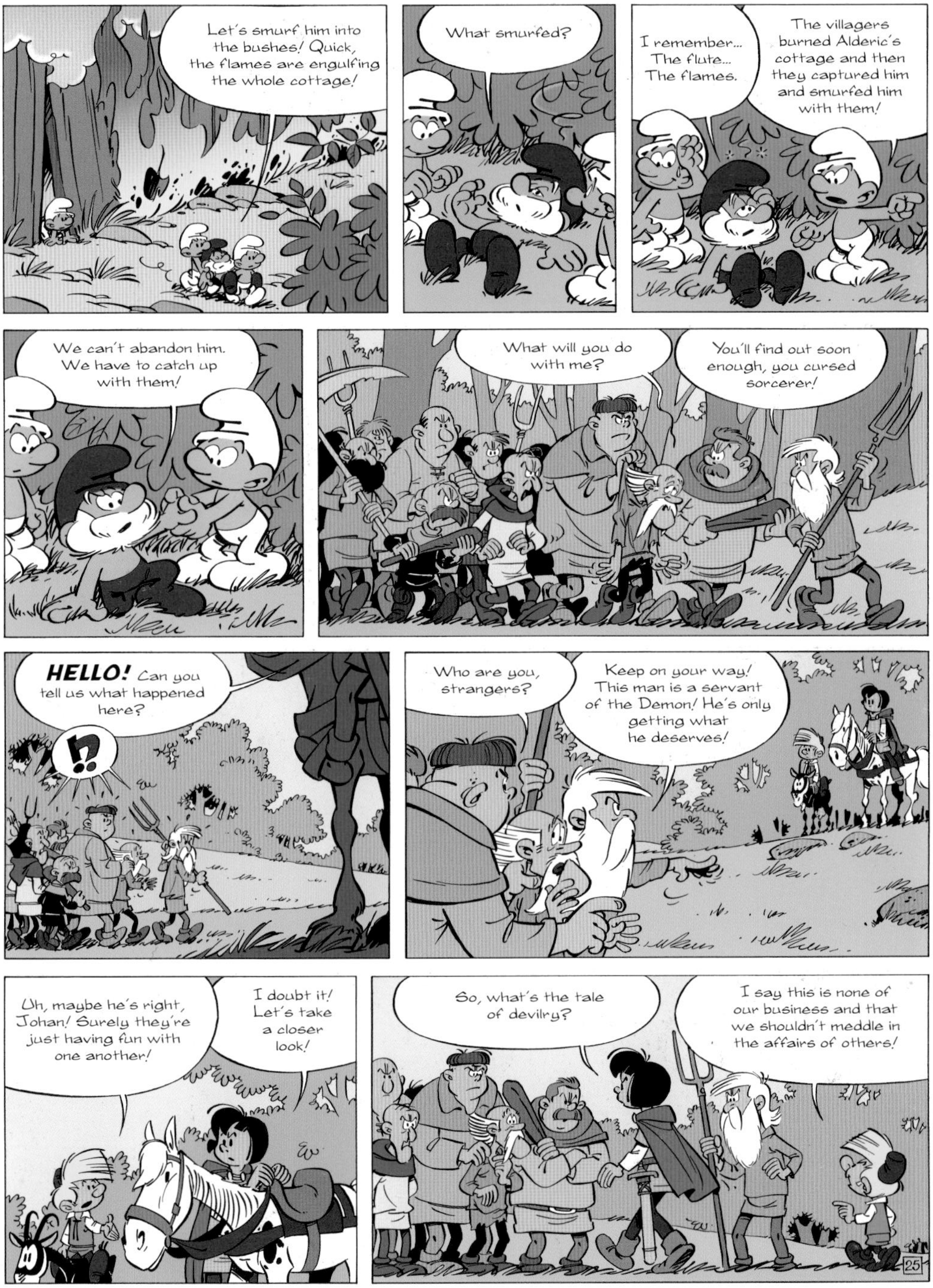
Let's smurf him into the bushes! Quick, the flames are engulfing the whole cottage!
What smurfed?
I remember... The flute... The flames.
The villagers burned Alderic's cottage and then they captured him and smurfed him with them!
We can't abandon him. We have to catch up with them!
What will you do with me?
You'll find out soon enough, you cursed sorcerer!
HELLO! Can you tell us what happened here?
!?
Who are you, strangers?
Keep on your way! This man is a servant of the Demon! He's only getting what he deserves!
Uh, maybe he's right, Johan! Surely they're just having fun with one another!
I doubt it! Let's take a closer look!
So, what's the tale of devilry?
I say this is none of our business and that we shouldn't meddle in the affairs of others!
25

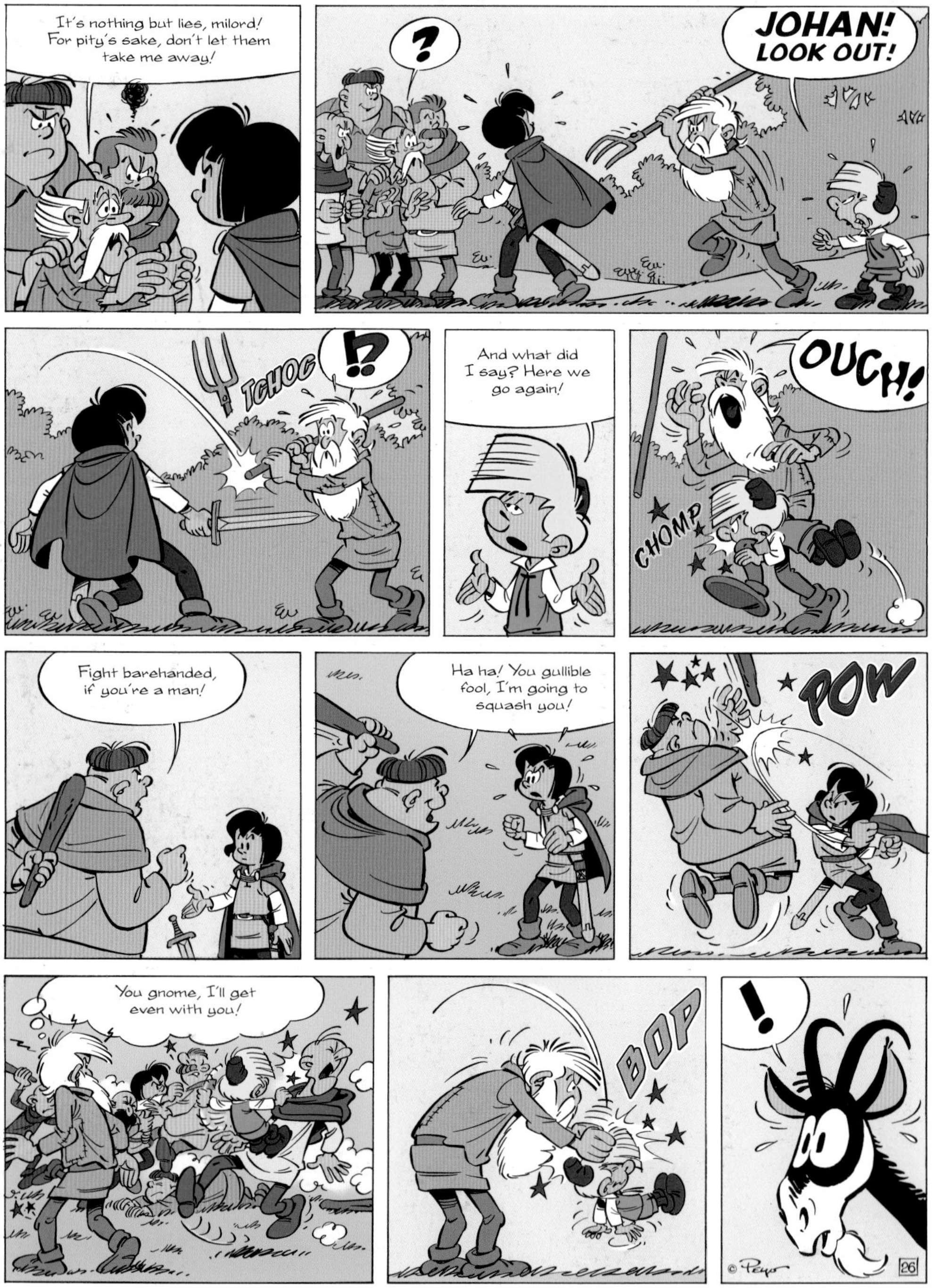

It's nothing but lies, milord! For pity's sake, don't let them take me away!
?
JOHAN! LOOK OUT!
TCHOC
!?
And what did I say? Here we go again!
OUCH!
CHOMP
Fight barehanded, if you're a man!
Ha ha! You gullible fool, I'm going to squash you!
POW
You gnome, I'll get even with you!
BOP
!
© Peyo
26

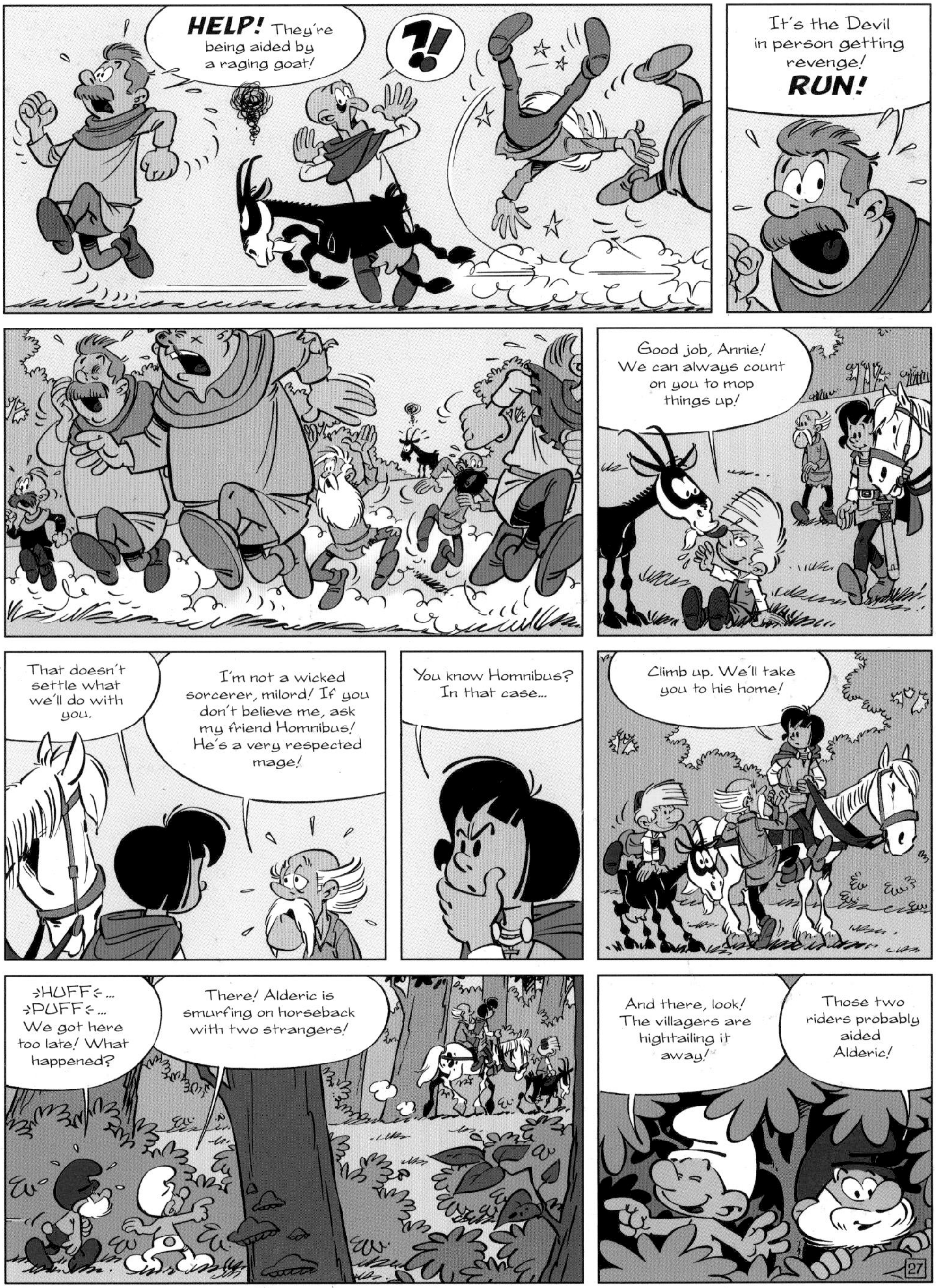
HELP! They're being aided by a raging goat!
?!
It's the Devil in person getting revenge! RUN!
Good job, Annie! We can always count on you to mop things up!
That doesn't settle what we'll do with you.
I'm not a wicked sorcerer, milord! If you don't believe me, ask my friend Homnibus! He's a very respected mage!
You know Homnibus? In that case...
Climb up. We'll take you to his home!
HUFF... PUFF... We got here too late! What happened?
There! Alderic is smurfing on horseback with two strangers!
And there, look! The villagers are hightailing it away!
Those two riders probably aided Alderic!
27

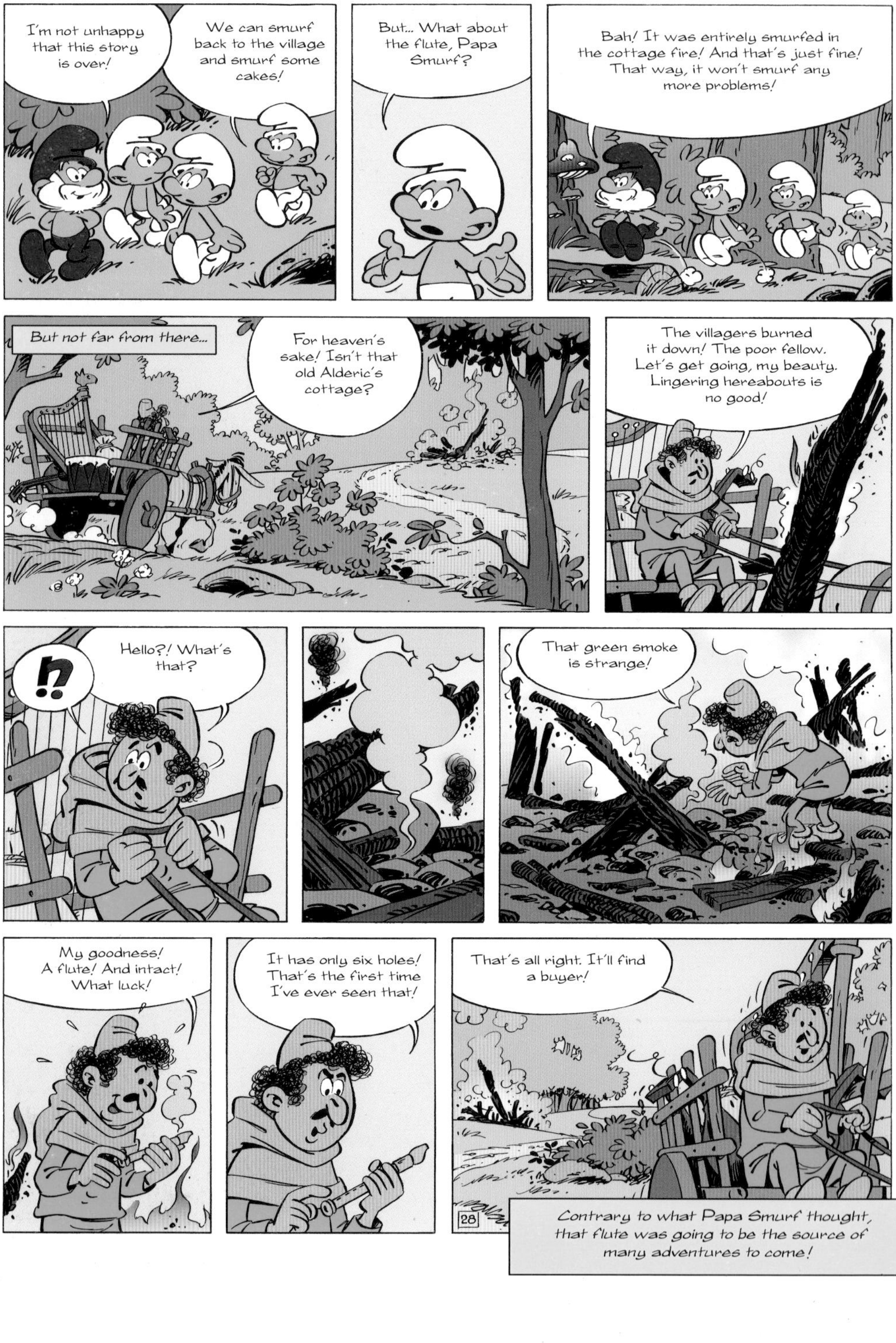
I'm not unhappy that this story is over!
We can smurf back to the village and smurf some cakes!
But... What about the flute, Papa Smurf?
Bah! It was entirely smurfed in the cottage fire! And that's just fine! That way, it won't smurf any more problems!
But not far from there...
For heaven's sake! Isn't that old Alderic's cottage?
The villagers burned it down! The poor fellow. Let's get going, my beauty. Lingering hereabouts is no good!
!?
Hello?! What's that?
That green smoke is strange!
My goodness! A flute! And intact! What luck!
It has only six holes! That's the first time I've ever seen that!
That's all right. It'll find a buyer!
28
Contrary to what Papa Smurf thought, that flute was going to be the source of many adventures to come!